CW00971336

Letters For Sarah

A Novel By
Susan Kay

PublishAmerica
Baltimore

First printing

ISBN: 1-59286-195-4
PUBLISHED BY PUBLISHAMERICA BOOK
PUBLISHERS
www.publishamerica.com
Baltimore

Printed in the United States of America

Dedication

My first book is dedicated to my husband,
Bill Thompson,
For his endless love and support,

And to our children,
Leann, Cindy, Dean, Jodi,
Who inspire me and remind me that
Nothing is more important than family!

Chapter One

1958

The tiny figure turned over to lie on her back against the cold, dirt floor. She slowly opened her eyes and couldn't help but squint from the bright sunbeam glaring through the small crack in the ceiling. It was the only light in the damp and dark cellar. At first she couldn't remember where she was, but the familiar, rancid smell of rotting potatoes made her realize she was in the old cellar once again.

Sarah June Taylor was eight years old but she felt much older than her young years. Her life was not one of a normal eight-year-old, although she didn't have much basis for comparison. She never had friends to play with and her only contact with other children had been in the church she attended with her parents each Sunday or at recess while she was in school. She always watched from a distance while the other children laughed and played. They seemed so happy. But Sarah did not understand happiness and only longed for the laughter and playfulness she saw in the other children. She was so shy and withdrawn that the other children thought she was odd and usually just left her alone.

After adjusting her eyes to the glare of the sunbeam, Sarah tried to stand up. She had been lying on the dirt floor with a couple of scratchy old potato sacks as her pillow. Her movement was slow and awkward as she pulled herself to her feet. The old familiar throbbing was there and she felt pain from her head to her toes. Hurting was part of her life, almost a daily routine now, except for Sundays when her parents took her to church. Sarah looked forward to Sundays.

She was on her feet now and moved cautiously to the door of the smelly old potato cellar. She took hold of the latch to open the door but hesitated when she heard her mother's voice in the distance. She didn't want her mother to see her until she was sure she had settled down from the earlier rage against her. When her mother's voice faded and Sarah knew she was gone, she tried to open the door but it wouldn't budge. Her mother had locked her inside. Again.

She let go of the door latch and sat down on an old orange crate. She couldn't do anything now but wait for her mother or father to let her out. What had caused the rage this time? What had she said or done to set her off? As her mind started to clear from the sleep, she thought back to breakfast that morning. Her mind replayed the scene.

****

The teapot whistled as Sarah entered the kitchen and sat down at the breakfast table. Her mother rushed to pull the boiling kettle from the stove and poured the hot water into the teacups for the morning tea. Sarah was just starting to eat her oatmeal when her mother sat the tea on the table. As Sarah reached for her glass of milk, she bumped her mother's arm and caused her to drop and break one of the teacups.

"You Idiot!" Her mother screamed. "Look what you've done! You've broken your grandmother's tea cup!"

Sarah winced and steadied herself for what she knew was coming. Her mother bent to pick up the broken pieces of the cup and as she tossed the pieces on the table Sarah saw her eyes flash with that familiar look of rage. Her powerful fist flew into Sarah's tiny cheek and she was knocked out of her chair to the floor.

"I'm sorry, Mother!" Sarah cried. "I didn't mean to do it. I'm sorry!" She pleaded as she curled into a protective ball on the kitchen floor. "Please don't hit me!"

But she knew her words were not heard because nothing stopped Alexis Taylor when she got like this. Sarah braced herself for the inevitable beating.

"You're stupid and clumsy!" Alexis screamed as she kicked Sarah.

"Always breaking my things!" Alexis' eyes had the look of a wild animal.

"Why did you have to be born? You're nothing but trouble!" She shouted as she kicked Sarah over and over in her ribs and back. Sarah crawled toward the kitchen door, trying to hold and protect her body as the kicking and yelling continued.

Sarah knew she must try to get away and give her mother time to settle down. She had seen her like this many times, but recently the frequency and intensity of the beatings were becoming unbearable. It was always the smallest of incidents that caused her mother to beat her. Maybe Sarah would understand someday. But for now, all she knew was she must be a very bad child to make her mother hate her so much. Her father, Harvey Taylor, wasn't much help to Sarah. He ignored his wife's yelling and screaming and spent most of his time at work or out in the barn when he was home. He didn't dare cross his wife and Sarah thought he must be afraid of her too.

Alexis continued to shout and throw things around the kitchen in her fit of rage. Her violet temper was working overtime now and anything in her path was in for trouble.

"Harvey!" Alexis yelled. "Get in here. You've got to do something about this brat."

She always tried to get Sarah's father involved as if she wanted his approval for her horrible behavior. Sarah heard her father's heavy work boots stomping toward the kitchen.

"What'd she do this time, Alexis?" He sighed with annoyance as he entered the room and saw Sarah lying on the floor, trying to mask the gentle sobs.

"She deliberately broke your mother's teacup and nearly scalded my arm." She lied.

Sarah expected her father to react to her Mother's provocation but he simply mumbled, shook his head, and scowled at Sarah. Sarah thought she caught a look of compassion in his eyes before he turned away and walked out of the house toward the barn with his head hanging down. He didn't dare challenge his wife for fear of making things worse and it was easier to walk away from the scene than to deal with it.

His lack of reaction only fueled the fire of his wife's temper and she jerked Sarah up from the floor, grabbed her tiny shoulders, and shook her hard. Sarah thought her head would leave her body from the force of the shaking and felt her teeth bite into her tongue. The taste of blood from her tongue made her feel nauseous as she tried unsuccessfully to push away from her hysterical mother.

"You'll think twice next time you decide to destroy my things! And this is just a sample of what you'll get if you ever do something like that again."

She jerked Sarah by her hair as she headed for the kitchen door. "Maybe some time in the cellar will teach you to respect other people's things."

Sarah was sobbing uncontrollably as her mother opened the door to the cellar and shoved her down the steps to the cold dirt floor.

"Don't come out until you've learned your lesson and are ready to apologize to me." She shouted.

The door slammed shut and Sarah was in the darkness. She hated the cellar. It was dark and damp and she knew there were bugs and spiders all around her. She felt something crawl across her leg and kicked in a panic to get it off. She couldn't see what it was but she really didn't want to see it and tried not to think about it. She was terrified of the old cellar and her mother knew this was the worst possibly punishment. She would rather suffer the beatings than be put in this cold, dark place.

Maybe if she tried to sleep, she would dream about something nice or at least not have to be aware of where she was for a while. So she closed her eyes and drifted off, still sobbing. She slept fitfully for a couple of hours; exhausted from the trauma and pain of the beating for something she hadn't meant to do.

****

She was startled when she heard someone outside the cellar and it sounded like someone was fumbling with the old lock. But, Sarah kept quiet. Within a few minutes, she heard the engine of their old pickup truck start up and knew her parents must be leaving. She reached for the latch once again. It had been unlocked. She carefully peeked out the door. She saw her father sitting at the steering wheel of his truck and her mother walking toward it. Maybe, if she hurried, she could make it to her room without being seen. She didn't want to upset her mother again.

But, she decided to just stay put. Why risk it? She would wait just a few more minutes until they were gone. She wished she could make her mother happy but she couldn't. She knew her mother did not want her or care about her. Even though she was only eight years old, she knew the meaning of love and she knew she was not loved.

Standing near and listening at the cellar door, Sarah could hear the sounds of the various farm animals. The animals were kept in the pen that connected to the big barn, just a few feet from the cellar.

Her family had one cow, they used for milking; two pigs that would be butchered later that fall for the winter's meat; and eight chickens that produced more eggs than the Taylor family could eat. The family dog was an old collie named Hank who slept most of the time and only barked when a strange car approached the house. Sarah's father said he was a good watch dog, but not good for anything else.

The Taylor home was an old weather beaten two-story house located about fifty feet from the potato cellar. It was badly in need of paint, just like the barn, the cellar and the fences. They had a big garden on the other side of the driveway and it was full of tomatoes, beans, corn and potatoes. Fruit trees lined the lane that extended out to the main road and served as a boundary for their property on the south side. The Taylor family grew most of their own food. The land helped them to be self-sufficient, and even though they didn't have much money, they always had plenty of food.

The old truck, with her parents inside, was now turning from their lane onto the main road that would take them to town. They couldn't see Sarah now, but she still darted quickly to the house.

Finally, safe in her bedroom, Sarah closed the door and curled up on the window seat where she could see the surrounding landscape. The Taylor's small farm consisted of twenty acres, fronting on the Snake River, and she could hear the sound of a waterfall off in the distance. Their property was about twelve miles from the tiny farming town of Benton, Idaho. Her parents had moved there before Sarah was born, just after her father's uncle died and left the house and property to Sarah's father.

She was an only child, which in Sarah's case, meant she was a lonely child. She was small for her age with long, white-blonde hair and huge, sad, blue eyes. She wore dresses every chance she got with ribbons to match tied into her hair. She was feminine through and through. Strangers who saw Sarah for the first time were enamored with her and drawn to her. They always commented on how darling she was and tried to get her to talk. But Sarah was very shy and afraid to speak to strangers, even when her parents were with her. She wasn't really afraid of the strangers, but afraid that she would say or do something to anger her mother. So, she would just smile when they spoke to her and nod her head.

She learned early on not to antagonize her parents in any way, especially her mother. She could not understand why strangers were so kind and attentive when her mother and father seemed to have no interest in her. She never heard the kind words from them that she heard from strangers. Her mother's words were usually spoken in anger, and most often to remind Sarah that she was bad or stupid. On the rare occasions her father spoke, it was usually in response to his wife's constant complaining. Sarah thought her mother must be right about her being stupid, so she tried to please both of them by keeping to herself and staying out of their way.

Sarah was born in June, in the year of 1950, in her parents' bed. They didn't have money for hospitals and doctors so Grandmother Sarah, her father's mother, helped with the delivery. The labor only lasted five hours and that was just long enough for Sarah's father to go get his mother to assist with the birth. Little Sarah's arrival to this world had been an easy one. She weighed five pounds, twelve ounces and was seventeen inches long. When Sarah was born, her paternal grandmother was thrilled!

"Look how beautiful and perfect she is, Alexis!" Grandmother Sarah said as she held her for Alexis to see. "What are you going to name her?"

Alexis was tired from childbirth and not happy about having a baby to care for.

"I really don't care, Mother Sarah. We didn't decide on any names. You and Harvey can decide. I'm tired. I'm going to sleep now."

With that, Alexis closed her eyes. She never even bothered to hold her newborn baby.

Grandmother Sarah was concerned about Alexis' lack of interest in her baby and expressed her concerns to her son.

"Oh, don't worry about Alexis," Harvey said nonchalantly. "She just needs a little time. Things like this are hard for her, Mom. She just doesn't know how to show much love. She needs time to adjust. It will be tough on her having to take care of a kid."

Grandmother Sarah was upset by what she had seen and heard, and felt sad for the darling little girl that lay sleeping in a dresser drawer. Her son and daughter-in-law had not prepared for the baby's arrival in any way and had no crib, diapers or clothes. She emptied the large bottom drawer from the dresser and placed a small blanket in the bottom to make a mattress. She tore a white sheet apart to make some diapers and brought used baby clothes from her neighbor. Without her efforts, the baby would have nothing. She had known Alexis was a troubled woman, and was not affectionate, but hoped this baby would bring out the maternal instinct in her daughter-in-law. So far, it didn't seem to make much of a difference. But, maybe Harvey was right. Maybe she just needed time to adjust.

"Harvey, what do you plan to name your baby?" Grandmother Sarah left her thoughts behind to focus on the task at hand.

Harvey paced back and forth, looking down at the sleeping infant. "Well, since you were here to bring her into the world, Mom, and you were the first person to see her, I think we should call her Sarah, after you. How does that sound?"

Grandmother Sarah loved the idea that the darling baby would have her name. "Thank you Harvey. I'd like that very much, if you think it is alright with Alexis."

"Oh, it will be fine. She told us to decide, didn't she?"

She smiled and gazed at the new little Sarah and said. "How about the middle name, Harv? Since she was born in June, how about you call her Sarah June?"

"Yeah, I guess that's a good name." He said as he shrugged his shoulders. "Sure, Sarah June Taylor."

Grandmother Sarah gazed at the baby with a puzzled look on her face. "Harvey, who do you think she looks like? She is so fair and it looks like her hair will be real blonde. She sure doesn't resemble our side of the family and I don't see any of her mother in her."

"Well, her looks must be from Alexis's side of the family somewhere. But who knows since we've never seen any of them. If this baby had been born in a hospital, I guess I'd be worried that they had given us the wrong baby." Harvey teased his mother.

Grandmother Sarah laughed, "Well, she sure is a pretty little thing, Harvey. You should be real proud of her." She picked up her sleeping namesake and kissed her cheek. "She is a darling."

For the next several years, Grandmother Sarah spent a lot of time taking care of little Sarah June. Alexis showed very little interest in her child and did only what was necessary to care for Sarah when Grandmother was not around to help. Grandmother Sarah never saw Alexis show any affection or attention to her child, and noticed the little one seemed afraid of her own mother. Harvey was more attentive but usually worked long hours and was so tired when he got home that he didn't have the energy to spend time with his child. So, in the first few years of Sarah's life, Grandmother Sarah was the only one who really cared for her.

Little Sarah June quickly learned her grandmother was the one who enjoyed spending time with her. She was the one who spent hours reading to her and rocking her in the big old rocking chair. Sarah loved cuddling into her grandmother's soft bosom. She was a chubby woman, and it was so comfortable to sit with her and fall asleep in her lap. Little Sarah looked forward to her frequent visits and she spent much of her early years at Grandmother's home. This was the person that taught Sarah June what it was like to love and be loved.

And then one day, Grandmother Sarah's visits stopped. Sarah was six years old when her father told that her Grandmother had gone to heaven to live with the angels. Sarah did not fully understand why Grandmother did not visit anymore, and her parents never explained anything further. She just thought she had done something bad to make her go away.

Life for Sarah, without Grandmother, was sad and lonely. It seemed her mother was always unhappy about something she had said or done, and her parents didn't talk to her or teach her things like her Grandmother had done. Her mother usually ignored her, but that was fine with Sarah. Having her attention meant she yelled at her or reminded her she was bad and stupid. And recently, the yelling had turned to slapping and beating. Now that Grandmother Sarah was gone, she had no one to turn to and worse yet, there was no one to hold her mother accountable. The abuse just got worse and worse. Sarah believed her mother would kill her one-day. Still, maybe death would be better than living in a world like this.

Now, as she sat in the window seat of her bedroom, overlooking the meandering Snake River, Sarah rubbed her swollen cheek and tears fell down her face as she thought of Grandmother Sarah. It had been two years since she died and it seemed so long ago. She missed her so much. At eight years old, Sarah thought bruises on her body were a normal part of life. She no longer remembered what it was like to be loved. She only knew she was lonely, and thought she must be a bad child that no one would ever want or love again.

Chapter Two

The house was quiet and the only sound was the peaceful and gentle movement of the river outside the bedroom window. Sarah lay on her bed reading one of her books. Before she died, Grandmother had brought boxes of used books for Sarah, and Sarah recalled her advice. "Sarah, when you want to escape from the world around you, just open a book and read. All of your troubles will disappear for awhile." She had been right. Reading was an escape for Sarah.

Sarah always remembered those words and she read every chance she got. She loved all kinds of books, and her second grade teacher had been impressed with Sarah's reading ability. She encouraged her by sending books home with her whenever possible. And now, even during the summer break, her teacher occasionally stopped by the Taylor home to bring more books to Sarah and help her prepare for third grade in September.

The books were such a happy place for Sarah. She read about travel and other parts of the world. She loved looking at pictures of paintings done by artists around the world. The colors and stories of the paintings fascinated her. She decided she would like to paint like that someday, and maybe even go to the strange and foreign places she read about in the travel books she found in the school library.

She tried to imitate the artists and used pencils to draw, and make the light and dark shades for the colors. She kept her sketches hidden in her closet, and hoped one day she could buy colored pencils so her drawings would look like the ones in the books.

After drawing and reading for a couple of hours, Sarah heard her father's truck coming down the lane to their home. Her parents had been gone all day, again. It was Saturday so her father didn't go to work at the meat packing plant, and usually took his wife somewhere on his day off. Sarah didn't know where they had been. They usually didn't tell her when they left, and Sarah never asked any more. She was used to being left alone, and almost preferred it now that she was older and didn't feel so frightened. They usually came home as is started to get dark outside and besides, she knew she was safer when they were away. She could read or draw all she wanted without being yelled at by her mother.

She hoped her mother had calmed down from the morning's beating and knew she would have to apologize even though she had done nothing wrong. After all, it was just an accident. But, Sarah had learned life was easier if she tried to please her. She heard the front door open and her parent's laughter as they entered the living room.

"Can you believe I won $25.00?" Alexis said cheerfully. "I'm going to buy that blue dress I saw in the window downtown at the Merc."

Sarah understood this was a rare good mood for her mother and sensed this might be a good time to talk to her. She tiptoed to the end of the hallway and leaned against the wall at the top of the stairs that led down to the living room. Listening to their conversation, she realized they had spent the afternoon gambling and drinking at the Blue Moon Bar again. Her mother liked the slot machines and bingo games, but usually came home complaining about losing the grocery money for the week. Her father played cards and had hot and cold streaks. Today had been a good day for them both, and Sarah was glad she didn't have to listen to the usual fighting that came after one of their trips to town. They both enjoyed the gambling, especially Alexis, and had gotten upset when they heard the gambling would soon be illegal in Idaho. They didn't see any harm in a little gambling.

The problem wasn't so much the gambling, even though they could not afford it, as it was the drinking that came with it. Sarah could tell they had both been drinking again. She never heard her parents laugh unless they had been drinking. She just hoped the drinking had not gone too far. A few drinks meant they were in a good mood. But, a few more meant the good mood could easily turn to a battle, and Sarah was usually the target for her mother's anger. She listened again to see if she could gage her mood.

"I came out a few dollars to the good on cards, so I'm going to treat us all to a picture show and dinner." Sarah's father sounded happy and said. "Alexis, go get Sarah and you two get ready to go."

Sarah thought this was the perfect time for her to join her parents, so she started to walk down the stairs as her mother argued, "Why do we have to take Sarah? Why can't she just stay here? I don't want her to spoil my fun tonight, Harvey".

"Alexis, we haven't left her at home at night before. Do you really think she is old enough to be by herself?" Her father questioned.

"She'll be fine, Harvey. I was practically on my own when I was her age. It's no big deal." Alexis continued, "Let her grow up and let me have a break for a change. I never get to have a good time."

Sarah stopped midway down the stairs and was frightened by what she had heard. She was going to be left alone, at night. Maybe her mother was still mad about this morning and that was the reason she didn't want to take Sarah with them. She decided she should apologize right away. She entered the living room and stood facing her parents now seated on the sofa.

"Hello Mother, hello Father." Sarah said quietly with her head bent down. She was afraid to look at her mother so she kept her eyes on her shoes and said, "Mother, I am sorry for breaking the teacup this morning. I will try to be more careful."

"You should be!" Her mother snapped as she stood up and walked toward the kitchen. "Now, get in here, I'll fix you some soup for supper. Your father and I are going out for awhile, and you're going to stay here."

Sarah looked to her father for help, but all he said was, "We'll bring Hank in the house to keep you company, Sarah. You'll be OK. Now eat your supper while we get ready to go."

The soup didn't taste good to Sarah as she thought about her parents leaving her at home, by herself, in the dark. She had never been home alone in the dark before, and she didn't like the idea. But she didn't have a choice. She didn't dare argue with her mother.

Alexis was twenty-nine years old and could be described as a little over weight. She wasn't very tall and looked heavier than she really was because of her height. She had dishwater blonde hair, about shoulder length, that usually looked dry and broken with no style. One could also describe her as pretty when she smiled, but Sarah rarely saw her smile, so she didn't see the pretty side of her mother. Rather she saw the captivating, blue eyes, full of hate and disappointment. She didn't know much about her mother's family or history, or what made her so full of hate. Her parents never seemed to talk about it. But, she remembered Grandmother Sarah telling her that Alexis had been abandoned when she was born and never knew her parents. Sarah knew she had been raised by numerous foster families and had a hard life going from one home to the other.

Grandmother told her, "Try to understand and be kind to her and love her. She had no one to love her when she was growing up."

Sarah remembered those words and thought, "At least I know my Grandmother Sarah loved me."

Her father came into the kitchen where Sarah was trying to eat her now cold soup and opened the back door. "Come in here, Hank!" He called. "Here boy!"

Hank came running to the door and hesitated. The dog was never brought into the house, so he was not sure what to do.

"Come in here, Hank". You're going to baby-sit tonight." Harvey said as he sat a bowl of water on the kitchen floor and watched as Hank lapped it up. When Hank was finished, he turned around and around not sure where to go.

"Sarah pushed her half eaten soup away and asked, "Can Hank come to my room with me, Father?"

"That will be fine for this evening, Sarah. I'll put him outside when we get home." He patted Sarah's head as he reached over to lock the kitchen door. "I'll lock the front door when we leave. You'll be fine."

Sarah watched him leave the room and thought, "Sometimes he acts like he really cares about me."

He could be kind at times, and his brown eyes had a softer look than his wife's eyes. Harvey looked like his father who had been slim and muscular with dark hair and olive skin. Sarah saw nothing of herself in her mother or father. She hoped she would be more like Grandmother Sarah, who had always been so happy and smiling. Sarah missed her so much.

Harvey grabbed two bottles of beer from the refrigerator and called out, "Come on, Alexis! Let's get going. It's already six o'clock, and we just have time to get some supper before the picture show starts."

"Coming! Just let me get my sweater." Alexis said cheerfully.

Sarah couldn't remember seeing her mother so happy. She had put her hair up into a French twist and looked very nice. Sarah wanted to be a part of the excitement.

"What will you see at the movie theater, Mother?"

"I don't know. What ever is playing I guess."

"Can't I please go with you?" Sarah pleaded.

"Movies are not for children." She snapped and glared at Sarah. All signs of happiness had left her face.

"Maybe next time, Sarah June." Her father said. "Now you take Hank and go to your room. Don't open the door to anyone. We will be home late, so you go on to sleep, and we'll see you in the morning. Hank will keep you company. Bye now."

Sarah's parents walked out the front door, locking it behind them. She ran to the living room window and watched as they got in the truck. Sarah thought they looked nice all dressed up. She seldom saw them without their old jeans and work shirts, but tonight Alexis wore a red skirt and matching sweater that made her hair look lighter and her eyes brighter. Her father wore new blue jeans with a dark green crew neck sweater. She looked so pretty, and he looked handsome, and they both looked happy for a change. It made Sarah feel happy too.

Now, alone in the old house near the river for the first time in the early evening, Sarah trembled as she walked up the stairs to her bedroom with Hank following behind.

"It will be OK, won't it Hank." She tried to convince herself. It's just for a little while, and I can read or draw. Anyway, I'll just pretend Mother and Father are here. We'll be OK."

From the window seat of her bedroom, Sarah watched the big, old winding river that seemed to come from the Owyhee Mountains in the background. It was summer in Idaho, and one of Sarah's favorite times. She loved the smells and sights of the surrounding farmland. In the distance, she saw the apple orchards, and just on the other side of the river, the cornfield was almost ready for harvest. Across the road from their property was a mint field. Even though she couldn't see the field from where she sat, she could smell it. Harvey told her the mint was used to make gum and Sarah thought the mint had a wonderful scent. She opened her window, as high as it would go, so she could enjoy the marvelous aroma.

Hank seemed uneasy about his new surroundings, so Sarah hopped up on her bed and patted her hand on the bedspread. "Come on, Hank. Come on up here with me."

Hank jumped up and lay next to Sarah and looked quite pleased. "It won't be so bad being alone." Sarah thought. "Hank will protect me."

Sarah picked up one of her Nancy Drew books, "*The Hidden Staircase*", and started to read. Nancy Drew was one of her favorite characters. She was so smart and pretty, and even had her own car. She was always solving some great mystery, and Sarah decided she would be like Nancy Drew when she grew up.

She lost herself in the story until she heard the old Grandfather clock chime and counted the strikes. It was nine o'clock. Summer in Idaho had long days, but Sarah realized the sun was almost gone. As the shadows reached across the room, she turned on her bedside lamp and looked out the window. The sun had dropped behind the distant mountain range. It would soon be dark, and she trembled at the thought. She quickly closed her window, then rushed to her bedroom door, slammed it shut, and pulled the latch to lock it. There, she felt better. She looked at Hank who was sleeping soundly. She thought, "Everything is okay. Hank isn't worried."

Sarah went to her dresser and pulled out her nightgown. She would try to get some sleep. She didn't know when her parents would be home, but thought she was too sleepy to wait and find out. As she removed her clothes, she glanced in the mirror above her dresser. She had some new, fresh bruises from this morning's beating that competed with some older bruises now fading away. Her cheek was swollen from her mother's fist, and her ribs were blackish-blue. She tried to see her backside, but could only see the sides of her thighs. They had the same blackish-blue marks.

Everything was tender to touch, but Sarah knew that would pass in a day or so. She gingerly slipped her nightgown over her head. Today's beating had been one of the worst she had experienced. It frightened Sarah to think about the way her mother looked when she beat her. She seemed so out of control.

Maybe someday she would learn how to make her parents happy, and her mother wouldn't beat her any more. She would try really hard to do that. She lay down, curled up next to Hank, and closed her eyes to welcome sleep. She whispered, "I'll try to make them happy. I'll try to be good, Hank. Really, I will."

Chapter Three

Sarah woke when Hank licked her faced and whimpered. She reached to pet him as he jumped from her bed and ran to the bedroom door. She sat up and rubbed her sleepy eyes. It was still dark outside and it took a minute for her to remember, she had been left at home alone. Hank scratched at her door and whimpered again.

"Do you need to go to the bathroom, Hank?" She asked, still in a sleepy haze.

Hank twirled around and barked as though he understood what she said. She unlocked her door and went into the hall past her parent's bedroom. The bed was empty. She was still alone. The clock chimed one o'clock as Sarah unlocked and opened the kitchen door to let Hank outside. She stood in the doorway and waited for him to come back, but instead Hank ran off and disappeared behind the barn. Sarah stood there in the dark, unsure of what she should do, and started to get uneasy. Now she was really alone, and Hank wasn't there to protect her. She quickly turned on the porch light. She was trying to decide if she wanted to go looking for him or just go back into the house when she saw headlights, and heard the sounds of a vehicle coming down the long lane that led to her house.

"Finally!" She said out loud to herself. "They're home." She breathed a sigh of relief and felt much better, until she looked closer. She realized the vehicle did not have the shape of her father's truck. Instead, it was a big, dark car, and it was coming closer and closer to the house. Now, Sarah was really afraid!

"Who could this be and what did they want?" She asked herself in a panic and all the questions raced through her mind. "What should I do? Where can I hide? Oh gee, where are my parents?"

She slowly moved out of the doorway, away from the light of the porch, and slipped her tiny body behind the overgrown shrub next to the kitchen door. She crouched down, so she could see the strange car without being seen. The car was moving slowly toward the house and would soon be at the barn. Sarah was so frightened she could barely breathe.

"Oh, where are they? Why aren't they home? And where is Hank?" She cried to herself as her eyes searched for him.

The car rolled to a stop, and the door opened. Sarah held her breath as she watched a very large man step out of the car and look around. Just then she heard a terrible, mean growl. Hank charged out from behind the barn and attacked the strange man. The angry dog took him by surprise and the man yelled and kicked at Hank to get him away from him. Each time the man managed to get free, Hank would attack again, tearing at the man's clothes and biting his arms and legs. Sarah had never seen Hank like this before. He was like a wild animal. The man managed to kick Hank and sent him tumbling a few feet away while he scrambled to the safety of his car and away from the angry and protective Hank. The car door slammed shut and the engine started with a roar.

Sarah couldn't believe what she had seen. Hank had protected her and chased the strange man away. The car went speeding back down the lane and turned onto the main road as Hank ran back to Sarah. She left the safety of the shrub and fell to her knees as Hank ran into her arms and licked her face over and over. She was safe. She grabbed Hank's collar and led him back into the house, locking the door behind them. Sarah and Hank went back to her bedroom and crawled into bed. Her little heart was pounding from the excitement, and she clung to Hank with both arms. "Who was that man and what did he want?" She asked herself over and over until she finally fell asleep again with Hank at her side.

When she woke the next morning, her bedroom door was open and Hank was gone, so she knew her parents were home. Today was Sunday, and she quickly dressed for Sunday school. This was her favorite day of the week. Her mother was usually in a good mood after church and that meant she didn't yell at Sarah. For some reason, her mother seemed nicer to Sarah on Sundays. And Sarah's father would be home all day. Maybe they would go fishing or hiking. She listened for the usual sounds coming from the kitchen and heard nothing but silence. She left her room and walked down the hall to her parents' bedroom as the clock chimed eight times. The door was closed, so she was hesitant. She was afraid to go in their bedroom after the incident last week and she stood at the door while her thoughts returned back to that day.

****

Alexis sat on the bed with her music box open, reading a letter. Sarah loved the sound of the music box and quietly stepped into her mother's room to listen. Alexis didn't see Sarah at first, and Sarah watched her as she sat staring at the letter in her hand. The music box had been a wedding gift from Harvey, and it was beautiful. It was dark wood that had been hand-carved with angels on the lid. It played the song *Edelweiss*. As she enjoyed the music, Sarah heard a sob from her mother and saw that she was crying.

"Mother, why are you crying?" She asked softly as she walked to the bed. She startled her.

"It's nothing." Alexis snapped as she wiped her eyes, quickly stuffed the letter into the music box and closed the lid.

Sarah was puzzled, and knew the letter must have upset her, so she asked as her curious hand touched the lid of the box.

"What is it, Mother? Why are you crying? Who was that letter from?"

"It's nothing for you to be concerned about, Sarah." She snapped again. Jerking the box from her, she said angrily, "Don't ever touch this box. These are my personal things, and they are none of your business." She inserted the key, locked the box, and placed it on the top of her dresser.

"You are never to come in my bedroom without permission. And don't ever sneak up on me again!" She yelled this time. "Now, get out of here."

****

Now, standing outside the door, she decided to knock lightly. She hoped they were awake because she had so much to tell them about last night. It seemed like a nightmare, now that it was daylight.

"Good morning." She said softly. "Are you awake?"

She heard her father moan as he replied, "Yeah Sarah, come in. What time is it?"

Sarah opened the door and slowly entered the room. "It's eight o'clock. It's time to get ready for church."

She glanced at her mother, not wanting to get in trouble again for being in their bedroom. Both her parents were in bed, and her mother was sleeping soundly.

"Shhh." Harvey whispered with his fingers to his lips. "Don't wake your mother. She isn't feeling so good."

Sarah had heard those words before, and knew that meant they had been drinking again. "If drinking made them feel so bad, why did they do it?" She thought to herself, as she looked at her snoring mother.

"We won't be going to church today, Sarah." Her father mumbled sleepily. "We need to sleep awhile longer. Now, go take off your good clothes and take care of the chores for me."

"But Father, I have to tell you something."

"Not now, Sarah." He interrupted. Now, go do what you're told."

Sarah knew better than to bother him again and went back to her room to change into her old clothes for doing chores. She struggled to pull on her old jeans that were now too small and grabbed the worn, flannel work shirt from the rack. She slipped on her beat up sneakers, and she was ready for work. Her father taught her what needed to be done each day for the animals, so she had no trouble taking care of them all by herself.

Her parents came downstairs about noon that day, and Alexis complained of a headache. Sarah decided it was best to stay out of their way, so she spent the day in her room reading her books and sketching with her pencil again. When her mother called her to supper that evening, Sarah decided she would tell them about the strange car and the big man Hank had chased away.

"Oh Sarah, you must have been dreaming." Alexis said with sarcasm. No one came here last night. Why would anyone bother? We don't have any thing worth stealing." Her mother tried to dismiss the story, but Sarah's father was very concerned.

"What did the car look like, Sarah? What color was it?"

Sarah hadn't seen the color in the darkness and only knew it was dark, big and long. She described what she could about the car and the strange man.

"Hank protected me! He bit him and tore his clothes and made the man get in his car and drive away really fast." Sarah recalled the events of last night with excitement and was relieved to realize that her father seemed to believe her story.

Harvey gazed out the kitchen window and said thoughtfully, "I think I know who came here last night, Alexis." The somber tone of his voice caught the attention of Sarah's mother.

"You mean you really believe someone was here, Harv?"

"It had to be Ben Jackson. He threatened to come here if I didn't get that loan paid on time. He means business. We've got to figure out a way to get him paid. I regret ever borrowing the money from him."

"We didn't have a choice and you know it, Harvey. Don't get so worked up about it. We'll get him paid somehow."

Sarah knew her father was worried, but her mother just shrugged it off. "Now, let's finish dinner so we can watch TV. *Bonanza* starts in a few minutes."

The Taylor family always watched *Bonanza* on Sunday evenings. They all sat together in the living room watching the popular television show while eating popcorn. Sarah's favorite character was *Little Joe*, played by Michael Landon. He was the youngest of three sons who lived with their father on a big ranch called *The Ponderosa*. Sarah thought he was so handsome and wanted to marry him someday when she was old enough. Her parents were always happy when they watched this show. It was one of Sarah's favorite times.

The week went by quickly. Alexis took Sarah to town with her to buy the new, blue dress from the Merc Department Store. She had been in a rare, good mood most of the week. And Sarah had gotten into trouble only one time after dropping the egg crate and causing some of the eggs to break.

"Sarah June!" Her mother yelled. "Those eggs were to be sold." She reacted quickly by slapping Sarah across the face, and then seemed to stop herself. "Why do you have to be so clumsy? We need that money from those eggs. You've got to be more careful."

Sarah was caught off guard and not sure what to think about her mother's reaction. She usually lost her temper and beat her over something like this. Maybe she was worried about paying back the loan, or maybe her good mood over buying the new dress had stayed with her. Sarah wished her mother could buy more dresses. It seemed she had become more and more unpredictable with her moods and Sarah was always on edge, not knowing what to expect from her mother.

When Saturday came, Harvey told Sarah about their plans to go out again and leave Sarah at home.

"We're going to leave Hank outside this time, Sarah. He's a good watchdog, and if Jackson comes back, Hank will get rid of him. You'll be okay in the house with the doors locked." He explained.

"Oh no, Father, please let Hank stay with me, in my room." Sarah pleaded. "I don't want to be alone."

"Nope, Sarah. Hank will just need to go out again, and it's safer for you not to open the door for any reason. Now, that's final!"

Sarah didn't argue with him. She sat in the living room waiting for them to get dressed up again to go out for the evening. And, as her parents drove away in the old pickup truck, she went to her room and locked the door. She would spend another evening alone.

Sarah was sound asleep when Hank's angry barking woke her. She crawled out of bed and looked out the window. It was dark outside but the glare from the moon let her see enough to know the old truck was not parked in the driveway. Her parents were still not home. She could not see Hank from where she stood, so she slowly opened her bedroom window and listened quietly. Hank's barking had stopped suddenly and she thought she heard a short yip from him. Then, there was silence. "Must have been barking at a rabbit." She thought sleepily and crawled back into bed. As she settled into her pillow, she heard the engine of a car. Just like the sound of the car from last week, the big car, with the big stranger. She froze with fear. Sarah was alone in the house, without Hank.

"He's back!" She barely whispered to herself. She was afraid to move for fear she would make noise, but she crept out of her bed again and cautiously looked out the window. This time she saw the big man walking toward the house and up the steps to the kitchen door. She wrapped herself into the long curtain so she would not be seen if he glanced upward to her window. She heard him try to open the door, but it wouldn't open. The lock was secure.

"What does he want?" Sarah cried to herself. "And where is Hank? Why doesn't he chase him away?" Sarah didn't see Hank anywhere.

"Taylor! This is Ben Jackson!" The big man yelled angrily as he pounded on the kitchen door. "I want my money!" He slurred his words, and Sarah realized he was drunk. "I've waited long enough and you're going to pay me." He kept pounding on the door. "I know you're in there, you son-of-a-bitch!" He mumbled and tried the lock again but it didn't give. "I'll be back! And next time I'll do more than get your dog." He shouted. Sarah watched as he stumbled down the steps and got into his car. His big car sped down the lane to the main road, where he turned toward town, and he was gone.

"What'd he mean, "get your dog", she thought in a panic. "What did he do to Hank?"

She ran to the corner of her room where she sat down with her knees curled to her chest and sobbed. She didn't know what to do. She was terrified and worried about Hank. She wanted to go outside and look for him, but was too afraid. What if the stranger came back? She sat in the dark, frozen with fear, for what seemed like hours.

When her parents finally came home, Sarah recognized the familiar sound of their truck and ran out of the house to meet them.

"He was here again!" She screamed as she ran to them. "He was here again!" She was crying hysterically now.

"Sarah, calm down and tell me what happened", Harvey said with concern as he put his arms around her. Alexis staggered after stepping down from the truck, and in her drunken stupor just stood next to Harvey, and tried to listen as Sarah quickly told them what had happened.

"Alexis, get Sarah in the house. I'll go look for Hank."

Sarah started to run after him, but he stopped her.

"No, Sarah! You go with Mother! Get in the house now!"

Sarah and Alexis went into the kitchen and sat at the table. Neither one spoke. Sarah could smell that awful smell on her mother. She was so drunk she had a hard time sitting upright in the chair, and she had a hard time focusing on Sarah.

In just a few minutes, Harvey came into the kitchen with a grim look on his face. "He's not fooling around, Alexis."

She just stared at him with a blank look on her face as if something did not register. "Who ya talkin' bout?" She slurred.

Harvey continued. "Ben Jackson. He means business this time, and he won't give up until he gets his money."

Sarah was starting to tremble. She knew something was really wrong and looked at her father anxiously. "Father, what about Hank? Is Hank alright?"

"No, Sarah, he's not." He hesitated, glanced at Alexis and then back at Sarah. "I'm sorry, Sarah. Hank is dead." He said softly as he put his arms around her and stroked her hair. "That mean SOB killed our dog. I found him laying out back of the barn."

"Oh no!" She sobbed as she clung to him. "Why did he have to kill Hank? Why?"

Harvey did not have an answer. He just continued to stroke her hair and hold her. "I'm sorry, Sarah. I'm so sorry."

Harvey turned to his wife and said, "Alexis, we've got to think of some way to pay him."

As Harvey picked Sarah up and started up the stairs to take her to bed she heard her mother mumble, "That mean ole bastard."

While her father helped her into bed, Sarah could smell that same awful smell of alcohol on him, just like her mother. She turned her head away so the smell would not be so strong. He tucked the covers around her shoulders and kissed her cheek.

"Good night, Sarah. Try not to cry anymore, and get some sleep. Tomorrow is Sunday School."

As he turned to leave the room, Sarah pleaded through her tears, "Father, please don't leave me alone at night any more. Hank can't protect me now. Please don't leave me alone again!" He didn't say anything, but just nodded as he slowly closed her door.

Sarah sobbed into her pillow. She cried for Hank. She cried for her Grandmother Sarah. She cried because she was only eight years old.

Chapter Four

Harvey and Alexis sat at the kitchen table, talking quietly and adding numbers over and over. The empty coffee cups sat off to the side of the table, and the note pad was covered with figures and scratches. They were frustrated.

"Alexis, we have to pay him somehow. Jackson's a mean man, and I've heard rumors of what happened to others who borrowed money from him and didn't pay. What he did to Hank is just the beginning." Harvey placed his head in his hands and sat with his shoulders slumped.

"Oh, Harvey, he's not that bad. You just worry too much. I guess we should have been born rich." Alexis said with sarcasm.

"Well, we weren't, so we'll just have to pay him somehow, or be prepared to suffer the consequences."

Harvey eyes went back to the notepad and he tapped his pencil on the table. "We can do it if we tighten our belts. We can get by with less and do without some of the extras for a while."

"What kind of extras are you talking about? We don't have any extras the way it is now!" Alexis was getting irritated. "We never have any extras, Harvey!"

"Well, I'll sell one of the pigs, and you can try to sell more eggs. And no more money for gambling and drinking until this is settled, Alexis." He scolded his wife.

"Now wait a minute, Harv. You can't expect me to give up everything. I'll cut down a little on the gambling, but I won't stop completely. That's not fair." She complained.

Harvey slammed his fist on the table and yelled. "Alexis, your damn gambling got us in this mess in the first place. With your reputation for gambling, I'm surprised anyone would loan us the money. Now, enough is enough. We just can't afford it, and you're gonna stop for awhile." Harvey got up from the table and as he opened the door to go outside, he turned and glared at his wife.

"Alexis, I mean what I say now, and that's final!"

Alexis knew how far to push her husband, and it was obvious that he would not back down on this issue.

"OK Harvey, I'll try." She whined. "All I can do is try."

For the next couple of weeks the Taylor family almost seemed like a normal family. Harvey went to work each day and came home on time, without stopping in town for a few drinks. Alexis stayed home, worked in the garden and started to freeze and can the vegetables she had grown. She left the house only to deliver the eggs she sold to the stores or neighbors. The refrigerator did not have any of the usual supply of beer inside, and Sarah was more at ease with her parents now that they had stopped drinking for a while. She didn't have to endure that awful smell of alcohol.

"Only a week or so, Alexis, and we will have enough money to pay him." Harvey said enthusiastically. He was at the kitchen table again with the notepad and pencil in hand. He counted the money they had saved and hidden in the kitchen cabinet.

"I talked with Jackson today and told him I would pay him in full in two weeks. He agreed, but said there would be no extensions. I assured him we wouldn't need any."

Sarah listened with concern as her parents discussed the big stranger. She knew he was mean, and she was frightened for her father. She was so glad her parents had not left her alone at night again. Now that Hank was dead, she was terrified to be alone.

Harvey continued. "The buyer will be here tomorrow to pay me for the pig, and I promise we will go out and celebrate when this is all over."

The possibility of going out again made Alexis happy, and she hummed while placing supper on the table. They sat down to eat fried chicken, sliced tomatoes, home fried potatoes, corn on the cob and peach cobbler for desert. In spite of her faults, Alexis was a great cook, and her family looked forward to her meals each day.

"After I get my paycheck, the end of next week, it looks like we'll have the money for him. We won't ever borrow money again, Alexis. I've been thinking a lot about this, and I think we need to stay away from the gambling and the bars. The gambling and drinking has caused us too much trouble."

Alexis laid her fork down and said, "Oh, Harvey, a little gambling doesn't hurt anybody. I'll just be more careful from now on." She looked at him with irritation and snapped, "We'll have Jackson out of our hair soon, so what's the big deal?"

"The big deal is that people like Jackson take action to get paid and I don't ever want to put my family in this situation again. We're just lucky that Hank was the only one hurt. He could have hurt Sarah too, you know!"

"He wouldn't do that, Harvey. And let's drop the subject. I'm sick of hearing about it, and I'm sick of staying home all the time. We haven't been out in weeks!" Alexis started to raise her voice. "I want to go somewhere tonight, Harv. After all, it is Saturday."

Sarah started to clear away the supper dishes as Alexis became more and more agitated with the conversation.

"Hurry and get out of here!" Sarah thought to herself. A little warning was going off, and Sarah knew her mother was losing control again. She had been too controlled for too long.

"It won't hurt us to spend a couple of dollars and go out for awhile, Harvey." Alexis said sweetly as her demeanor suddenly changed again. She moved closer to Harvey, sat on his lap and ran her fingers through his hair.

"We're not going anywhere until that debt is paid in full and that's final, Alexis!" Harvey shoved Alexis away from him. "This conversation is over!" He shouted as his fist slammed into the wall leaving a hole in the plaster.

Sarah was terrified and stood in the corner, afraid to move. Now, both parents were mad and yelling at the other. She didn't want to be in the room with them and tried to stay out of their way. Not wanting to irritate them further, she decided to finish the dishes while they argued. When their yelling slowed down, Sarah softly said, "Mother,

I'm finished with my chores. May I go to my room to read?"

"No you can't, you lazy brat! That's all you do is read, read, read." That dreaded wild look was in her eyes again. "If you want to read so bad, read this!" Her mother screamed as she picked up a newspaper, lying near the table, and smacked Sarah in the face.

Alexis was now out of control. Using the newspaper, she continued to strike over and over, while Sarah did her best to protect her face and eyes with her hands. As the beating caused the paper to fly apart, her mother became more enraged and reached for the cut firewood piled in the box near the door.

She struck Sarah on her back with the wood and shouted. "You're lazy and no good." Sarah collapsed and gasped with pain.

As Alexis drew back to hit a second time, Harvey grabbed her arm and yelled. "Stop it, Alexis! Sarah didn't do anything wrong." He wrestled the wood from his wife. "You're not going to beat the poor kid for nothing this time. I've had enough of your temper."

Sarah didn't wait to hear the rest of the conversation. She ran out the kitchen door as fast as she could. She ran to the old barn into the tiny room where the grain was stored. She could hide here until the fighting stopped. She could hear the yelling and screaming coming from the kitchen, and she covered her ears with her hands and sat down on the grain sacks sobbing. Her face stung from the beating, and she felt like her back was broken from the sharp whack of the firewood.

"How could her mother be so cruel? Why did her parents have to fight so much?" She cried to herself, "Everything had been going so good. Why did her mother have such a temper? Why did she hate her so much?" The questions came easily, but the answers did not.

Sarah stayed in the old barn until it started to get dark. Everything seemed quiet now, so she slowly went back to the house, entered the dark kitchen, and tiptoed up to her room. Sarah's father was not in the house and Sarah assumed he had taken a walk down by the river. Her mother must have been in her room because Sarah noticed the door was closed. Sarah slipped into her nightgown, went to the bathroom and placed a cool cloth on her swollen face. Her back ached and she could feel a huge tender knot where the firewood had struck.

"Oh well." She sighed. "It will feel better tomorrow."

She crawled into bed and as sleep came to Sarah, a slight smile came to her lips.

"Tomorrow is Sunday. It will be a nice day!" She thought happily and drifted off to sleep.

Sunday morning, as she woke and got out of bed, she heard her parents downstairs in the kitchen talking about a picnic after church.

"We can take the boat across the river and have a picnic on the island." Alexis said cheerfully.

"I'll take the fishing gear for me and Sarah." Harvey added. "We'll catch some trout for dinner tonight."

"Thank goodness. They're in a good mood." Sarah said to herself. She quickly dressed, combed her hair and went downstairs for breakfast.

"Looks like you're ready for church, Sarah June." Her father said cheerfully as he looked up from the newspaper and his cup of coffee. There was no mention of the problems from the night before.

"Eat your pancakes, Sarah. We need to leave soon." Her mother said, without that enthusiasm Sarah had heard in her voice before she came downstairs. Sarah just seemed to always make her mother unhappy. She had to try harder to be good.

Sarah always enjoyed Sunday school, and today was especially fun. Her teacher, Mrs. Peterman, told the class the story of Jacob and his coat of many colors. She let the children draw and color pictures to go with the story and told Sarah her drawing was the best of the class. As a prize, Sarah was given a tiny Bible, and after class was over Mrs. Peterman pulled Sarah to her side and said, with concern, "Sarah, what happened to your face, Honey? It looks a little swollen and bruised."

"Nothing," Sarah said shyly as she looked around to see if her parents were near. "Really Mrs. Peterman, nothing happened."

"Well, okay then." Mrs. Peterman said suspiciously, knowing Sarah had not been truthful. "But Sarah, if you ever need a friend, you can call me, you know. Anytime, okay?"

She wrote her phone number on a piece of paper and placed it in Sarah's new Bible. "This is my home telephone number. Don't forget, Sarah. You can call me anytime."

"Thank you, Mrs. Peterman," Sarah replied, as she gazed into the kind face of her teacher for a moment before she walked away.

Mrs. Peterman was a nice young woman who was married to the local banker and lived in town. She was tall and slender with soft brown eyes and short brown hair. She always looked so neat with everything in its place. She was twenty-five years old and was going to college to become a schoolteacher. Sarah thought she would be a good schoolteacher because she was such a good Sunday school teacher. She loved the children, and frequently brought little gifts or treats for them.

Mrs. Peterman talked to her class as if they were her friends. She told them she did not have children of her own, so she usually volunteered at the school and taught Sunday school classes, just so she could be around children. She had only one more year before she would graduate and become an elementary school teacher. Sarah secretly hoped she would be her teacher at school one day.

Sarah thought she was a wonderful lady and looked forward to seeing her each Sunday. Today had been the first time she had taken Sarah aside to ask about her, and it frightened Sarah a little. She didn't want anyone to know what happened. She didn't want to get in trouble, and it never occurred to Sarah that she could tell someone about the abuse she suffered so she could get help. Even though she was nervous about Mrs. Peterman questioning her, Sarah felt good. This was the first time, since Grandmother Sarah had died, that Sarah knew she had a friend, and that someone cared about her. So today, life was good.

Chapter Five

The Taylor family went on their picnic and caught fish that day, just as they had planned. It was a beautiful summer day in late August, and Sarah couldn't remember a better day with her parents.

"This is the way families should be." She thought, "No yelling or screaming, no slapping or beating. Mother and Father actually smiling and talking without fighting. Yeah, this is the way it should be."

School was scheduled to start soon, and Sarah looked forward to third grade. She had already heard about her teacher from the children in her Sunday school class. They all thought she was nice, but sent homework with them and required the students to read several books during the school year. As the children complained, Sarah thought to herself. "What's wrong with having to read books? I think third grade sounds fun!"

Sarah's grades had been very good in her first two years of school. Most of the time she was the top student of the class, but she didn't like for the other kids to know that. It made her feel even more different. She dreaded the times the teacher singled her out for getting good grades, because the kids teased her and called her Smarty Pants. She liked to study and learn, and didn't understand why the other children complained about it so much.

Today the girls in Sunday school class talked about their school clothes and how excited they were to show off the new purchases. Sarah knew she would get her school clothes from the Salvation Army store again. But it was okay that they were used clothes, they were still new to her. She needed to remind her mother that school would start soon, and they needed to get her school clothes and supplies. As Sarah's family returned from the picnic that evening, Sarah brought up the subject.

"Mother, school starts next week. When can we go shopping for my school clothes and stuff?"

"There won't be any shopping this month, Sarah." Alexis replied with a faraway look in her eyes. "Maybe next month we will have the extra money."

"Right now all of our money will be used to pay Jackson, Sarah." Harvey added. "You'll have to get along with what clothes and supplies you have for awhile."

Sarah was disappointed and wondered what she would do without paper and pencils for school, but she knew this was not the time to ask. Today had been such a nice day with no yelling or fighting, and she didn't want it to change. She would think about school later. Right now she was hungry.

"Father, I'll help clean the fish for dinner."

She took the string of trout out to the barn and started cleaning. Her father had taught her how to clean them, and she was proud of herself for learning. She always caught more fish than he did and loved to tease him about it. She didn't even mind handling the worms, and when she told the girls at church about it, they all turned up their noses.

"Yuk, Sarah." One of the older girls said. "Fishing is for boys."

"Yeah Sarah." Another added. "It's so messy and smelly. Why would you want to fish? You are so weird!"

"I think it's fun." Sarah replied and quickly realized she had given the girls another reason to think she was different from them. The girls looked at her like she was crazy and walked away.

Sarah felt embarrassed for just a moment and then shrugged her shoulders. She didn't care. They were just sissies. She liked to fish, and besides, it was fun to go fishing with her father. He always seemed so happy while he fished and told her stories about when he was growing up. She loved to hear about his childhood, and it made her feel good to hear about Grandmother Sarah again.

He had been born and raised in Idaho and was also an only child. His father had died in a farming accident while Harvey was still in high school. Harvey and his mother had been very close until just after his graduation from high school when he started dating Alexis. She had moved in with a foster family that lived next door, so she spent a lot of time at the Taylor house.

Harvey's mother did not approve of Alexis and was worried about her moody behavior. But Harvey fell in love with her, and his mother learned to accept her into their lives. Harvey told Sarah that Alexis had lots of boyfriends, but when they started dating she gave up all the other guys for him, and they soon got married. Sarah had been born six months later, but Sarah's father did not tell her that part of the story. She had figured that out on her own, and Grandmother Sarah had confirmed she was right.

The week passed quickly, and Sarah was excited knowing school would start the following Monday. Harvey brought her a small tablet and two pencils.

"This will get you started until we can afford to buy the rest of your school supplies. I'm sorry we can't do more, Sarah."

Alexis had been unusually quiet all week. She hardly spoke to Sarah, but seemed very loving and attentive to Harvey. Sarah wondered about the strange behavior and when Saturday afternoon came, she knew what her mother had been up to.

"Harv, how about we go to town for just a drink or two? I need to unwind and get away from here. Just for a while, Honey?" She said sweetly and tilted her head as though she were shy. "We won't be gone long."

"I don't want to leave Sarah by herself, Alexis. She is afraid now that Hank is gone." Harvey said with concern. "Besides, I want to pay Jackson before we spend money on anything extra."

"I know, but I made a little extra selling eggs this week and Harvey," she pleaded now and smiled a seductive smile. "We could use a little time to ourselves, if you know what I mean."

She glanced at Sarah and continued. "Sarah will be okay for a little while. We'll only be gone for an hour or so. I promise, just one drink, and we'll come home. You'll be okay, won't you, Sarah?" She said while giving Sarah a look that said, "Don't you dare cross me."

Sarah nodded her head and quietly said, "Yeah, I'll be fine."

"Well, all right, Alexis." Harvey gave in. "As long as it's only for an hour or two. I guess we could both use a change of scenery. Go get ready, so we can get home before it gets dark."

Alexis went up to her room, and Sarah felt the terror of being alone again as her tiny body started to tremble.

"What if that man comes back, Father? What will I do?" She said as her voice quivered.

"He won't, Sarah. We won't be gone long." He assured her. "Just keep the doors locked. You'll be okay."

It was seven o'clock when her parents left the house. Sarah had calmed down by then, knowing it wouldn't be dark for at least another hour. She curled up in the same old rocking chair Grandmother Sarah had used to rock her as a baby and started reading her book. After a while, when she started to get sleepy, she lay down on the sofa and went to sleep.

She woke with a start when she heard her father's angry voice. He yelled at Alexis as she stumbled through the door. Sarah didn't know what time it was, but knew it was late. Her mother had been drinking again and was obviously very drunk.

"I should have known better than to let you talk me into going out." He screamed. "How could you do it, Alexis? Do you have any idea what you've done?"

Sarah thought he must be mad at her for making him stay gone so long after promising Sarah they wouldn't be late. Alexis slumped into the chair and tried to focus her eyes on Harvey as she slurred her words.

"I didn't mean to lose it, Harv. I thought I was on a roll. I didn't mean to lose it, Harv. Really I didn't!"

She was pleading with him now, and Sarah saw anger in her father's eyes like she had never seen before. They hadn't even noticed Sarah was in the room. She quietly got up and went to the curve of the staircase where her parents wouldn't see her, but she could still see them. She didn't understand what her mother had lost and why her father was so mad. But she thought it would be safe to sit on the stairs and just listen until she found out why they were so upset.

Harvey went to the kitchen cabinet and took down the jar that had held the precious money. It was completely empty. He came back to the living room where his wife sat crying with her head in her hands. He threw the glass jar across the room and it smashed into the fireplace, shattering on the hearth and floor. He paced the floor with his fists clenched and glared at his wife. Sarah gathered her knees to her chest in terror while she watched and listened.

"It's bad enough that your gambling got us into such a mess that we had to borrow money from that crook, but it's unforgivable that you took every damn penny we had saved to pay him back and gambled it away!"

Sarah immediately stiffened. Now, she realized what this fight was about. Her thoughts raced. "Mother had lost *that* money, the money from the sale of the pig. The money they had saved for weeks now. The money that could have bought Sarah's school clothes and supplies. The money from the cabinet was all gone! That meant Jackson would not get paid! And that meant he would be back!" Sarah sat on the stairs, watching her parents, and wondering how her mother could do such a horrible thing.

Harvey jerked Alexis up from her chair and screamed, "I'll never forgive you for this! Never!" Alexis looked terrified but said nothing. "I've put up with your lying and your problems long enough! If you hadn't been pregnant, I never would have married you."

Assuming Sarah had gone to bed, it never occurred to Harvey that she might be listening. He threw his wife to the sofa and started to walk away. But in her drunken stupor, Alexis did not know when to leave well enough alone. Her temper flared this time as she yelled. "Well I certainly wouldn't have married you if I hadn't been pregnant. I don't even know if you're her father."

Harvey lunged at Alexis and hit her over and over. Sarah had never seen him so upset. He was like a madman, yelling and crying at the same time.

"Don't ever say that again." He screamed through his tears.

"Please stop!" Alexis pleaded. "I didn't mean it, Harv!"

But Harvey didn't stop. Alexis was now on the floor and curled up to protect herself just like she had caused Sarah to do so many times. Sarah was unable to react for a moment. She watched her beg him to stop beating her, just like she had begged her mother to stop beating her so many times before. And then she couldn't stand it any more.

"Please stop, Father." Sarah cried as she left her hiding spot and rushed to him. "Please stop! You're hurting her!"

The sound of Sarah's tiny, terrified voice brought Harvey back to his senses, and he stopped the beating and let his wife slump to the floor. He stood in the living room with tears on his face and mumbled.

"I, I'm sorry, Sarah. I'm sorry I lost my temper."

He looked down at Alexis who was sobbing on the floor and softly said, "I'll never forgive you for this, Alexis."

He walked out of the house, and Sarah saw him go into the barn.

Alexis pulled herself up from the floor and stumbled up the stairs to her bedroom. Sarah stood in the living room for a while trying to understand what all this meant. She knew that night had changed things for her family, but she couldn't know just how much.

It was Saturday night. Maybe things would be better on Sunday. Things were always better on Sundays. She climbed the stairs to her room and stopped at her mother's closed bedroom door. She could hear her crying, and wished she could do something to make her feel better.

"Mother, are you alright?" She asked while choking back her own tears. She knew how bad she must feel right now.

"Please don't cry, Mother. Every thing will be okay." Sarah tried to reassure her as she stood outside the door.

But Sarah knew it would not be okay. Her mother had done a terrible thing. Still, she felt she must try to make her feel better.

"I love you, Mother." She said, hoping to hear something from inside. And the reply finally came from a voice that sounded far away, and like one of a stranger, not her mother.

"Good night, Sarah." She replied.

Sarah stood still, not sure if she should leave her alone but afraid to bother her.

"Sarah." Her mother said softly and Sarah could hear the sobbing in her voice. "Come in here, Sarah."

Sarah opened the door and entered her mother's room. "Yes, Mother?" She spoke softly, uncertain why her mother had called her into her room.

Alexis lay on the bed holding her music box, and staring at the ceiling. Sarah moved closer to the bed as Alexis turned to look at her. Her eyes were glassy and red from crying. Her face showed no expression or emotion as she spoke to her daughter.

"There is no such thing as love, Sarah. Don't ever forget that." Alexis turned away again and Sarah knew she wanted to be left alone.

As Sarah walked away and into her own room, she realized her mother had never told her she loved her. And now, she understood why. Her mother did not believe in love. Grandmother Sarah had told Sarah how much she loved her many times, and told her how important it was to tell others that you love them. Sarah wished her grandmother could be here, so she could talk to her mother and tell her about love. But Sarah knew that could never happen. Grandmother was gone. And maybe Grandmother had been wrong, maybe there really was no such thing as love. Sarah hadn't felt loved in a long time.

That night, Sarah slept fitfully. Her mother's words stayed in her head as she tossed and turned.

She woke early the next morning, and without getting dressed, ran downstairs. She wanted to see her mother. Maybe everything would be better today, and maybe her mother would feel differently. It was Sunday, and it was a beautiful day. She would be extra good, so her mother wouldn't get upset with her. And, she hoped her father had settled down. After all, they would work out the problem of paying that Jackson man some how.

Sarah rushed to the kitchen, but stopped when she saw her father sitting at the table. Something was not right. There was no breakfast on the table, and there was no coffee cup or newspaper in front of him. There was no teapot on the stove for Sarah and her mother. Her father looked up at Sarah. There was a letter in his hand and tears were spilling down his cheeks. Sarah had never seen him like this, and walked slowly to his outstretched arms.

"What's wrong, Father?" Sarah felt panicky.

He buried his face in her hair and sobbed, "What have I done, Sarah, oh what have I done?"

As he held Sarah tight, the letter fell to the floor. She recognized her mother's handwriting, but couldn't see the words. Harvey quickly retrieved the letter and stuffed it in his shirt pocket. Sarah was confused and frightened.

"What do you mean, Father? What's wrong?"

"It's your mother." He replied slowly and so softly, Sarah barely heard. His eyes held hers for a second before he continued.

"She took too many pills." His voice was trembling. "I slept in the barn last night and I found her this morning." He hesitated, patted his shirt pocket, and as a sob caught in his throat said, "She left this letter. She's dead, Sarah. Your mom is dead."

Chapter Six

Sarah didn't know most of the people who came to the Taylor home that day, but she had seen some of them at Sunday School and knew some of them worked with her father from the conversations she overheard. She watched from the curve in the staircase as the sheriff talked to her father for a long time in the living room. They were both seated on the sofa facing the stairs. She couldn't hear their words, but watched as her father held his head in his hands and cried openly. The sheriff patted his back as if to console him, but it didn't seem to help. It broke her heart to watch him. She had never seen him cry before, and she didn't know how to help him. She felt so helpless, not knowing what to do or what to say, so she just sat on the stairs and leaned her head against the wall.

Mrs. Peterman arrived, and sensing the mood, quickly took charge of the Taylor home. She fixed tea and coffee for Sarah and Harvey, tidied up the house, and helped Sarah get dressed. She didn't talk much or ask questions, she just hugged Sarah and tried to comfort her with her actions rather than words. She understood Sarah didn't need to hear words right now. Words were meaningless to her, and the hugs were what Sarah needed more than anything.

After the Taylor home was in order and Harvey and Sarah were settled, Mrs. Peterman made several phone calls to arrange for church members and friends to bring food for Harvey and Sarah. They came with their gifts of sympathy, and by mid-afternoon the table was covered with chicken, ham, casseroles and deserts.

Sarah vaguely remembered the women fussing about her and hugging her. They brought plates of food for her to eat but she couldn't eat anything. She was amazed that all those people could be in her kitchen eating and talking. Didn't they know an awful thing had happened? Shouldn't people stop eating and talking and just think about this awful thing? Shouldn't every thing be different now?

As soon as the sheriff concluded his business and drove away, Sarah went to her father and put her arms around him. Now that she could be close to him again, Sarah held on to his arm, not really hearing or seeing anything that went on around her. She was afraid that if she didn't hold on to him he would go away, just like her mother. It just didn't seem possible that her mother was dead and that Sarah would never see her again.

Sarah did not start school on Monday with the rest of her third grade class, and her father did not go to work. Together they made arrangements for the funeral. She felt numb and had no feelings or emotions. She wanted only to be with her father and refused to leave his side. Her world had turned to a blur after hearing her mother was dead.

The funeral service was short, and only a few people attended. Sarah's mother had no family, and only a few friends from town. Most of the people who attended were members of the church, or her father's co-workers, who were there to show support for Harvey and Sarah. And, of course, Mr. and Mrs. Peterman came. They sat directly behind Sarah, and Harvey and Sarah turned around to try and smile at Mrs. Peterman as they took their seats.

Sarah glanced around the chapel and saw the familiar faces. It made Sarah feel good to know these people cared enough to attend the services. She thought she recognized everyone in the room today, but as her eyes drifted to the back of the chapel, she saw an unfamiliar face. She knew she had not seen this tiny older woman before, yet she had a strange feeling that she knew her. The woman was well dressed and was very pretty. Her image stayed with Sarah, and several times during the service Sarah turned around only to see the woman staring at her. Sarah seemed drawn to her, but she did not understand why. She should have been uneasy that this stranger kept staring at her, but Sarah wasn't uneasy. She was just very curious about this kind looking lady.

As the services concluded, she decided to ask her father about the woman. She wanted to know if he recognized her. So as they walked out of the church, she pointed to the woman who was now standing in the church parking lot, watching them.

"Father, who is that lady?" She asked just as Mr. and Mrs. Peterman approached them, and Harvey didn't have a chance to look. Sarah lost sight of her and turned her attention to Petermans.

"Harvey, we are so sorry for your loss." Mrs. Peterman said as she took his hand.

"Yes. Please let us know if there is anything we can do." Mr. Peterman added.

"Thank you." Harvey replied. "I appreciate that."

Mrs. Peterman turned to Sarah and knelt down to put her arms around her. "I am so sorry, Sarah." She said quietly and with damp eyes.

Sarah hugged her tightly, and for the first time gently sobbed into her chest. Mrs. Peterman held her tight and stroked her hair for a few minutes. Then she pulled Sarah from her chest and looked directly into her sad eyes and added.

"Something like this is so hard to understand. Maybe you never will understand. But I want you to remember I am your friend and I will always be there when you need me. Please remember that, Sarah."

"I will." Sarah nodded as Mrs. Peterman hugged her once again, and then took her husband's hand and walked away.

As Sarah turned to search for the strange lady, she saw her slowly approaching. She came within a couple of feet of Sarah and Harvey, and reached out as if to touch Sarah. She looked into Sarah's eyes and smiled. Standing with his back to the woman, Harvey did not see her approaching and put his arm around Sarah to lead her away. The woman started to speak, as if to stop them from leaving, than hesitated.

As Sarah and Harvey walked away, Sarah turned and watched her walk back to the parking lot and get into a shiny, expensive looking car. Their eyes locked one more time for a brief moment as the lady smiled again, waved to Sarah, and drove away.

"Who was that lady, Father?" Sarah asked again as her car went past Sarah and Harvey.

"I have no idea, Sarah. Must be a member of the church."

Harvey did not give her another thought, but Sarah did. She could not get her out of her thoughts and knew there was something familiar in those huge, sad, blue eyes.

Later in the week, Sarah's father took her to school for the first time on his way back to work. It was time to try to get the family back to a normal routine. Sarah had lost all excitement for third grade, and her father barely spoke anymore. There was so much sadness in their home, and neither father nor daughter knew how to handle it. She knew her father felt responsible for her mother's death. He had told Sarah how Alexis committed suicide after their horrible fight. Sarah wished she could have done something to make her mother feel better that night. Both were racked with their own guilt, and their silence compounded the sadness.

One week passed, and there had been very little communication between Harvey and Sarah. Sarah sat at the kitchen window watching the slow moving river and noticed her father sitting on a log next to the riverbank. She felt so alone and wanted to be near him. She wanted to talk to him and wanted him to talk to her. She wanted to go fishing again, or something. Anything, just so they could be together and she wouldn't be so lonely. Sarah didn't miss the yelling and beatings from her mother, but she did miss the simple everyday chatter. The house was so quiet now.

She slowly walked down to the river and sat next to him on the log. Neither spoke for several minutes until finally he broke the silence.

"There's some things you should know about your mother, Sarah." He starred at the river as though looking for the right words and continued.

"Alexis was never a happy person. No matter what I did or said, it wasn't good enough. I took her to doctors, but it didn't do any good."

"What was wrong, Father?" Sarah asked, thinking her mother must have been sick.

"The doctors said she was real depressed, because of her childhood and all. You know, her mother abandoned her when she was born, and Alexis seemed to hate the world because of it. She never knew anything about her real family and would never talk about it. She was so bitter all those years, and it turned her into a mean person. She tried taking medication for a few years just after you were born, but it didn't help much. She quit taking it a couple of years ago and refused to even talk about getting help for her problems."

Sarah's grandmother had told her a little about her mother's childhood, but she listened intently while her father told her what happened in more detail.

"She was passed from one foster family to the next all her life. Most of the time she only stayed for a month or two before she was sent on. She never felt like anyone cared about her, and I suppose she never learned much about caring for other people. She had too much hate in her. I guess not having a family that loved her made her the way she was."

Harvey looked at his daughter and hesitated before continuing.

"She threatened to kill herself a couple of times, Sarah, and one time she even tried to do it right after you were born. But I thought she just wanted attention, and I never thought she would actually go through with it. She was a sick woman, and once she started the drinking and gambling, it just made things worse for her and all of us."

He turned to look at Sarah now, and she thought she had never seen such sorrow in his face. He put his arm around her and pulled her close to him.

"She never was much of a mother to you Sarah, and I'm real sorry about that. I guess I haven't been much of a father either. But I'll try to make it up to you somehow. You see, Honey, your mother never should have had children with her mental problems and all. I guess I thought she would change and learn to be a good mother when you were born, but she never did. She just couldn't do it. She just didn't have it in her. Your grandmother tried to warn me about her, and the problems she had, but I couldn't see it. I loved her and wanted to make her life better. I thought I could make her happy, but I never did.

"Why did she beat me so much? Did she hate me?"

"No Honey, she didn't hate you. She just didn't know how to love you."

"Why did she have to put me in the cellar. I hated the cellar."

"I know you did, and that's why I used to unlock the door when she wasn't looking, so you could get out. But I should have done more. I should have stopped her, but I never wanted to upset her. I'm sorry for the way she treated you. I wouldn't blame you if you hated her, and me, for what has happened."

Sarah thought about all the beatings, the screaming and yelling, which had occurred so frequently, especially after Grandmother died. Then, she thought of those few good days she had with her mother and her final words, *"There is no such thing as love, Sarah. Don't ever forget that."*

It seemed a long time ago now, and Sarah just could not feel hate for her. She just felt sad for her, and sad for her father. She took his tanned, rough hand and held it between her tiny hands.

"I don't hate her. Grandmother Sarah told me Mother never had anyone to love her, and that I should love her a lot to make up for that."

"You know Sarah, your grandmother was a wise woman." Her father took her in his arms.

"Alexis' heart was so full of hate she didn't have much room for love, but I'm sure she loved you in her own way, and so do I."

"I love you too, Father."

They talked a lot that day about Alexis, and how they both felt, and Sarah felt much better afterward. They seemed to open up some invisible closed door that had kept them apart. He talked to her as he would to another adult, instead of a child, and shared things that helped Sarah understand her mother and the horrible behavior.

She wasn't afraid to share her feelings with him now. She was worried about Ben Jackson, and expressed her concerns to him as they ate supper together that evening.

"Father, if all the money is gone, how will you pay him?"

"I've been thinking about that all evening and we really don't have a lot of choices. We'll have to sell the other pig and the cow to raise the money. Even with that, I still can't pay the whole loan."

"I'm afraid of him." She said remembering what he had done to Hank, and the sound of his mean voice as he pounded on their door.

"I know, Sarah, but I don't know what else to do." He said as he shook his head. "I had to borrow money from my boss to pay for the funeral. And now he will take the money from my weekly paycheck until that loan is paid. Things are going to be real tight for awhile."

"When do you have to pay him?" She asked.

"I promised him I would pay this week, and my time is already past due. I have to think of something. It looks like there won't be any school supplies or new clothes for you, Sarah."

"That's okay." She replied as she wondered what she would do without a winter coat. "We'll get by somehow. Just please pay that awful man!" She pleaded.

During the next couple of days, Harvey managed to find a buyer for the livestock, and he sat at the kitchen table counting the proceeds from the sale.

"I have enough here to pay him almost half of what's owed." He explained to Sarah. "I'm going to meet with him and see if I can work something out." He grabbed his dusty old cowboy hat and headed out the kitchen door. "I'll be back."

Harvey stood in Ben Jackson's office and handed over the money he had counted earlier.

"I'm here just as I said I would be." Harvey said nervously as he turned his hat over and over in his hands.

"You're a couple of days late and it looks like you're a little short, Taylor." Jackson grumbled as he counted the money for the second time.

"I know. I wish I could keep my promise to pay you in full today, but I can't. I came to ask you for an extension."

"I told you there would be no extensions, Harvey." Jackson snapped.

"I know that too, Ben, but you see we had most of the money saved up to pay you before my wife died. I had to use some of it to give her a funeral. I still have half for you. Now, I'm asking you to give me an extension."

Harvey straightened his back, and said it with a matter of fact attitude. He didn't tell Jackson what really happened to the money. He didn't want him or anyone to know his wife had gambled it all away. Jackson looked at him and neither man spoke for a moment.

"Sorry about Alexis, Harvey." Jackson said with just a touch of compassion this time. "I felt real bad when I heard about it. How is the kid?"

"She's doing all right." Harvey replied.

"Tell you what. I'm feeling generous today. I'll give you that extension. But I want the balance paid by the first of the year, no later. That gives you more than three months to come up with the money."

"Thank you, Ben." Harvey said.

"I'm only doing this because I feel sorry for the kid, Taylor. And this is a warning to ya." He added with all signs of compassion gone, "You had better come through this time. I've let this go way too long. I'll take action if I need to."

Harvey had no doubt this man was capable of carrying out his threat, and he felt his anger start to rise. He clenched his fists but held his tongue knowing he would only cause more problems by challenging him. He quickly said. "You'll get your money." He turned to leave the room.

"Taylor, there won't be any more extensions." Jackson warned again as Harvey closed the door behind him, placed his hat back on and breathed a sigh of relief.

"Well, I got the extension!" Harvey thought to himself as he started the engine and headed for home.

"But how in hell will I raise the money in three months?" He said out loud this time. "There's nothing left to sell."

Harvey felt years younger now that Jackson was taken care of for a few months. Things were finally looking up. He would worry about the money later. Right now he just wanted to take care of Sarah and try to be a good father for a change. He was all she had now and she was all he had. She was his only family.

Sarah slowly adjusted to school again, even though her grades had suffered for a while, she soon caught up with her class. The students and teachers all seemed to be nicer to her, but Sarah knew they felt sorry for her, because she didn't have a mother.

Mrs. Peterman stopped in to see the Taylors every few days, and usually brought some kind of cake or cookies for them. One day she came to visit, and this time brought a huge box and a sack.

"I had some left over supplies from my college classes and thought you might like to have them."

She lied to Sarah, and didn't tell her she had made a special trip to purchase the needed school supplies. Mrs. Peterman had dropped in at school, earlier that week, to visit Sarah's teacher and asked how Sarah was doing. The teacher told her Sarah needed a few items and was concerned that she didn't have many clothes. It didn't take long for Mrs. Peterman to take care of the problem.

"Thank you, Mrs. Peterman!" Sarah exclaimed as she removed tablets, pencils, erasers, and crayons from the sack.

"What's in the box?"

"Oh, just a few things my niece outgrew, and I thought they might fit you, so I hope you don't mind if I give them to you."

She directed her comment to Harvey, not sure how he felt about charity. But Harvey was touched by her kindness, knowing he could not provide the things Sarah needed.

"Thank you very much, Mrs. Peterman. I'm sure Sarah can use everything. Tell your niece thank you for us."

"Yes, thank you." Sarah added as she removed several dresses, underwear, shoes and even a winter coat in just her size.

"Things are looking up!" Harvey said to himself as he thanked Mrs. Peterman once more and saw her to the door.

Sarah couldn't remember when she had been so happy. She had her school supplies, just like the other students, and she had stacks of nice clothes to wear to school.

The Taylors were getting along just fine. Harvey was quiet most of the time, but that was just his way, and Sarah understood he was a man of few words. She did all she could to make him happy and she knew he was trying to do what was best for her. The lack of interest he had shown in Sarah for so many years now seemed gone. It had been buried with his wife. He seemed to be a different person, now that Alexis was dead. Sometimes, he sat and starred into space for long periods of time and didn't always respond to Sarah when she spoke, but she understood he was lonely and missed his wife. Sarah missed her too some times, but she didn't miss the beatings, and she didn't miss the fighting. Life was a little sad and lonely for them at times now, but in many ways it was so much better.

Chapter Seven

As winter descended, Sarah and Harvey settled into a comfortable routine as he went to work and she went to school. He tended to the chores and chopped firewood, while she cleaned the house and washed their clothes. Each evening, as they fixed their supper together, they talked about their day and shared stories. Harvey even started to take an interest in Sarah's schoolwork and sat with her while she did her homework.

Sarah started to blossom. She wasn't afraid to talk to him anymore, and she learned so much about him from their evening chats. He seemed kinder now and very protective of her. She had not been beaten or yelled at since her mother died, and she even sang and skipped around the house while she did her chores.

Harvey noticed the change in Sarah and was pleased to see she was so happy. He thought it was sad she hadn't felt happiness while her mother was alive. But he knew Alexis had caused Sarah to be unhappy and frightened. Even though he missed his wife, he had come to believe some things happen for a reason and maybe he had to suffer the loss of his wife before he could be a good father to his daughter. Sarah was his whole world, and he wanted to make up for the terrible things she lived with in her first eight years.

Mrs. Peterman continued to drop by and check on Sarah and Harvey every week, and they became good friends. Sarah liked talking to her about school, and Mrs. Peterman often helped Sarah with her homework. She was so good to Sarah and always hugged her when she came to visit. Sarah knew she would finish college in the spring and would be a teacher next year. She hoped she would teach at her school next year, or better yet, be her teacher in fourth grade.

When Christmas arrived, it was both happy and sad for Sarah

and Harvey. Sarah missed her mother's cooking and making the Christmas decorations. She tried to remember how to make things the way her mother had made them, and with her father's help, they decorated the tree in time for Christmas morning. Sarah made an ashtray for her father at school and wrapped it in paper. He was touched by her efforts and hugged her tightly.

"Thank you very much, Honey. This is great! It's even big enough to hold my pipe."

Harvey stood up and walked to the door.

"I'll be right back. Your present is in the barn. Close your eyes and don't look until I tell you."

Sarah covered her eyes and sat waiting on the green sofa, next to the Christmas tree until she heard the door open.

"Okay, Sarah. Open your eyes. Merry Christmas!"

Sarah squealed with delight as Harvey handed her a darling puppy. It was a Black Labrador with a beautiful shiny coat and big paws. Sarah fell in love instantly.

"He's so cute! Thank you so much, Father!" She hugged and kissed her father as the new puppy squirmed and licked her face.

"How old is he and what's his name?" She asked as she rubbed his shiny coat. She was thrilled with her gift and the puppy was just as excited with his new owner.

"He's six weeks old and just left his mother. His name is Jake!"

"Can he stay in the house with us, Father? It's too cold for him outside." It had been snowing for days and the snow was two and three feet high in places.

"That's fine for tonight, but remember he is an outside dog and belongs in the barn at night. We don't want to spoil him. He is your responsibility now, and he's not house broken yet, so you'll have to watch him real close and put him outside when he needs it."

"Don't worry, Father, I'll take good care of him. Thank you so much!"

He was just what Sarah had hoped for since that awful man had killed Hank. She didn't want to leave Jake alone, and for the next few days, Sarah and Jake were inseparable. Jake followed her everywhere. Even though Jake was supposed to stay outside or in the barn during the day, she insisted he be in the house with her all the time. Harvey tried to get him to stay outside, but both Sarah and Jake whined until Harvey finally gave in.

Sarah thought her life was good now. She was excelling in school and was the top student of the class again. She had her father, Mrs. Peterman and Jake and she was very happy.

Then, one Friday night, just after the New Year, the telephone rang at the Taylor home and Sarah answered.

"Taylor residence. Sarah speaking."

"Give a message to your father." It was a deep, gruff voice that sent fear through her body. She immediately recognized the voice of Ben Jackson.

"Tell him, time's up!" The phone line went dead.

Sarah stood holding the phone and staring at her father.

"Who was it, Sarah?" Harvey said with concern when he saw the look on her face.

"It was that man." She said as she trembled and thought of what he had done to Hank. She rushed to Jake who was lying on the floor in front of the warm fireplace and knelt down to rub his shiny fur.

"Who do you mean, Sarah? What are you talking about?"

Sarah repeated the message to her father and said. "Do you have the money to pay him?"

Harvey stood up and clenched his fists. He started pacing the floor. "No Sarah, I don't have the money to pay him. I had to pay the property taxes this month and with my boss taking the money from my paycheck every week, I haven't been able to save enough to pay him."

"What are we going to do?"

"I don't know, Sarah. I just don't know." He said thoughtfully and tried to reassure her. "But you don't worry about it. I'll think of something. Maybe he will settle for some of it." Harvey knew the chances were slim that Ben Jackson would settle for any thing less than what was due, but he didn't want Sarah to worry.

The following evening, the telephone rang again. This time Harvey answered.

"Taylor residence."

"Didn't you get my message, Taylor? Time's up! The money is due, and I want it now!"

"Where can I meet you?"

"Blue Moon Bar. Be there in half an hour."

"I'll be there."

Harvey hung up the phone and turned to Sarah. "I need to go into town for awhile. Take Jake up to your room while I'm gone."

"Who was that on the phone?" Sarah asked with concern. Her father was acting strange.

"Just a friend, Sarah." Harvey lied. "He needs me to help him with something. I'll be right back."

"Don't go, Father, please don't go. I don't want to be here by myself. It's dark outside." She pleaded with him and knew something was not right.

"Sarah, just lock the door behind me. You'll be fine."

Sarah remembered how her mother and father used to drink and gamble and she felt the panic set in.

"Please don't drink, Father." She felt like a baby with the way she was acting, but she was afraid for him to go. She had not been left alone at night since her mother had died, and Jake couldn't protect her. He was just a puppy.

Harvey put his arms around her. "Sarah," he said softly as he took hold of her shoulders and looked into her eyes, "Don't worry. Everything will be fine."

He kissed the top of her head and reached for his coat and hat. Sarah watched as he drove the old red Ford pickup truck down the snow covered lane and turned onto the main highway. It was six o'clock on Saturday evening when Sarah closed and locked the front door just as her father told her to do.

She took Jake up to her room and decided she would sketch to keep her mind occupied. She tried to draw Jake, but he wouldn't lie still, and she finally gave up. Her father had been gone for more than three hours now, but she was sleepy and was sure he would be home soon. She crawled into bed and with Jake curled up next to her and fell asleep.

The sound of the rooster, crowing from the barnyard, woke Sarah and Jake at six o'clock Sunday morning. She jumped out of bed knowing Jake should be let outside before he had an accident. As she passed her father's room, she noticed the bed was made. It wasn't unusual for him to be up this early, but he seldom made his bed until after breakfast. She went downstairs to let Jake out, and then called out to her father. But, there was no answer, and she assumed he must be outside doing the chores. She quickly ran out to the barn to find him, but he was not there. Then she realized his truck was not parked in the driveway.

"I'll bet he just went to town to get the morning newspaper." She told herself. "I'll just fix breakfast, and he will be here soon."

Sarah fixed coffee and pancakes, just like her father had taught her to do, and sat eating hers at the kitchen table while she waited and watched for her father from the kitchen window. It was now eight o'clock and he was still not home. It was time to get ready for church, so Sarah got dressed and continued to wait on the front porch. The sun was shining, and it was a nice January day. The snow was melting, and it was warmer than normal for this time of year.

But church time came and went with no sign of Harvey. Now, Sarah was worried. Something was wrong. They had not missed church since Alexis died more than four months ago.

She tried to think back to last evening and remember what he had said about the phone call. He didn't say where he was going and only mentioned a friend, but not a name, so Sarah did not know where to look for him or what to do.

It occurred to her that her father may not have come home last night, and she had been alone all night. She paced the floor just as she had watched her father do so many times and wondered what she should do. She forced herself to sit down on the sofa and read her book to take her mind off of her worries, but found it was hard to concentrate.

Maybe she should call someone, but whom would she call? Then she remembered the tiny Bible she had received from Mrs. Peterman. She got the Bible from her room and opened it to find the piece of paper with the telephone number for Mrs. Peterman.

"I'll call her." Sarah said to Jake as though he would answer her and tell her it was a good idea. "She will know what to do."

Sarah felt better as she dialed the number to the Peterman home. But the phone just rang and rang. No one was home. The clock showed Sarah it was eleven o'clock. Her new friend would just be getting out of church, and she remembered Mrs. Peterman always had Sunday dinner with her parents right after church. But, Sarah did not know how to reach Mrs. Peterman's parents. She placed the receiver on the cradle and sat down with Jake curled up next to her.

"There is nothing to do but wait."

Chapter Eight

It was nine o'clock Sunday evening as John and Carol Peterman left her parent's house and headed for their home on the edge of town. They had enjoyed a great Sunday dinner with Carol's family. All five of her brothers and sisters had been there with all nineteen nieces and nephews. John and Carol were exhausted from the long, fun filled day full of games, eating and talking with all of the family members. Carol sat with her head resting on the seat of the car and was deep in thought.

"You seem distant, Carol. Is something on your mind?"

"Well, actually I have been concerned about Sarah Taylor and her father. They didn't come to church today, and I can't help but wonder if everything is okay. It's just not like them to miss church."

"I'm sure its nothing, Honey. They probably went fishing. Harvey talks about it all the time and claims he never gets enough time to go, so he probably did. Don't worry so much. You worry about everything."

He teased her, knowing that was what made her so special and he loved her for it. Carol was always the first one to help neighbors or friends when they needed anything. She was devoted to her students at church and loved them as if they were her own. She was a wonderful woman, and John felt bad they couldn't have children of their own. But after four years of marriage and numerous visits to doctors, they had realized it wasn't meant to be. Recently she had started to talk about adoption, and John had agreed to think about it. He wanted her to be happy, and he knew she would be a great mother.

"I can't help it, John." She tried to sound light-hearted. John was right. It seemed she was always worried about someone or something.

"But I do worry about Sarah. She is such a special little girl, and she has been through so much after losing her mother that way. Maybe I'll call her when we get home."

"I know you have become attached to Sarah. But Carol, this is a school night, and I'm sure she will be in bed by the time we get home. I doubt her father would appreciate a phone call this time of night." John gently scolded.

"You're right. It's probably nothing but my overactive imagination working again." Carol agreed as she looked out the car window in the darkness.

At the same time, Sarah was dialing the telephone to the Peterman home. Again, the phone rang and rang. She had called all day and when she returned the receiver this time, she cried to herself.

"I don't know who else to call, Jake." She said tearfully as she hugged Jake to her.

Her father had been gone for more than twenty-four hours, and Sarah was sick with worry. She was too worried to go upstairs to her bedroom. She wanted to be close to the telephone in case her father called so she curled up on the sofa in the living room.

"He probably had trouble with that old truck again. He'll be home soon. I'm sure of it, Jake." Jake snuggled next to her and as they drifted off to sleep for the second night Sarah wished Grandmother Sarah could be with her. She would know what to do.

****

Ed Foster and Jerry Barker were fishing at the big bend of the Snake River, midway between town and the Taylor property, just as the sun rose Monday morning. The main road followed the river as it made the bend, but the road climbed up a small hill and left the river down below. It was a favorite fishing spot and the local fisherman had left the road so many times to get to the water, the ruts had become well worn. No one ventured down without a four-wheel drive vehicle, and this time of year was especially difficult traveling with the melting snow and mud. Ed and Jerry made the trip frequently and had arrived this morning while it was still near dark. They parked on the flat beach area near the river's edge.

Ed was already frustrated with his poor results and reeled in his fishing line. Jerry caught a fourteen-inch trout and was giving Ed a hard time about it. They were both competitive when it came to their fishing, and Ed wasn't about to be out fished today. He walked down the bank of the river until he found what looked like a good fishing hole just off the bank, though it was still a little too dark to see real well. As he cast the line, the reel jammed and wouldn't release the hook and sinkers for the normal casting distance, and instead made a plop into the water just a few feet from the shore. He cursed as he started to reel in so he could try again. But as he reeled, the line caught tight. This time it caught on something and made a strange sound like the tackle had hit metal.

"What the heck was that, Ed?" Jerry heard the same unusual sound and saw Ed struggling with his fishing pole.

"Must be something in the water, but I can't see what it is."

"What ever it is wasn't here a couple of days ago. I fished the very spot you're in now and nothing was in the water, but that big old trout I had for dinner." Jerry teased as Ed struggled to free his tackle. "Serves you right for stealing my spot, anyway!"

As the two men walked closer to the edge of the water, the reflection of the sun hit just right on a metal object sticking out of the river.

As the sun continued to climb into the sky, the two men were able to see what looked like a tailgate of a red pickup truck. It was imprinted with Ford.

"I'll be darned." Ed said as he shook his head.

"I think we'd better forget the fishing, Ed. Let's go get the sheriff."

****

Carol Peterman woke at dawn. She had tossed and turned all night from worry about Sarah. John was already dressed and ready to leave for his office as Carol came into the kitchen.

"You're up early, Honey." He said as he kissed her cheek.

"I know, John, but I just have to call the Taylors and see if everything is alright." Carol reached for the telephone and started to dial. "I know it's early but I can't wait any longer."

A sleepy Sarah picked up the telephone. "Hullo." It took her a minute to focus on her situation.

"Sarah, this is Mrs. Peterman. Are you......"

Sarah was instantly awake. "Oh, Mrs. Peterman!" She cried. "I called and called yesterday, and you weren't home. My father didn't come home and I don't know what to do!"

"Sarah! Have you been there alone all night?" Carol asked in a panic and looked to John as she spoke.

"Uh huh." Sarah was starting to sob now. "H-he has b-been gone two n-nights. I don't know w-where he is."

"Sarah," Carol tried to say in a soft, calm voice, "I'll be there as quickly as I can. Don't worry, Sweetheart, I'm on my way."

John had heard the conversation and said, "I'll drive you, Carol. Go get ready while I call my secretary to let her know I may be late coming in."

Carol rushed to pull on a pair of Levis and a warm sweatshirt while John started the car and scraped the ice from the windshield. Within minutes they were on their way to Sarah. Sarah opened the front door and ran to Carol as the Petermans got out of their car.

"Oh, Sarah! Are you all right?" Carol held her tight and stroked her long hair. "I'm so sorry you couldn't reach me. You've been here alone for two nights? Thank God, you're okay!"

Sarah clung to Carol as they went into the house. John called the sheriff's office, which took the information and said they would call back, while Carol fixed breakfast. Carol was terrified for Sarah's father and felt responsible for Sarah.

Harvey had been missing for two days, and Sarah only knew he was going to town and had said something about helping a friend. She told the Petermans all she knew about the disappearance of her father, which wasn't much, while Carol served breakfast. John and Carol sat at the table and drank coffee while Sarah just moved the food around on her plate without eating.

"Sarah, please try to eat. I know you are worried but you have to eat something."

Sarah had not eaten since Sunday morning when she made the pancakes her father never came home to eat. She had been so worried and terrified afterwards that she never thought to eat again. Now she felt sick at her stomach, and a huge knot seemed to be growing there from the fear she felt. Carol tried to comfort and reassure her, but even Carol was afraid. She knew something had gone terribly wrong.

The sheriff's office called John and told him the sheriff would be at the Taylor place right away. Sarah had just managed to finish a bit of breakfast, and Carol was clearing the dishes as the sheriff's car turned from the main road onto the Taylor's lane. John went outside to greet him as Carol stood with Sarah and watched from the kitchen window. As the two men talked Carol could tell by the expression on her husband's face that the news was not good.

John was a composed businessman, used to dealing with people's problems and situations, but telling Sarah what happened to her father was the hardest thing he had ever done. Two fishermen had found the old Ford truck in the icy Snake River, just a short while ago. Harvey had apparently hit a patch of ice and missed the turn where the road curved along the river. The truck and Harvey Taylor had apparently plunged into the river Saturday evening. Sarah's father had drowned.

So, before Sarah had turned nine years old, she had lost her Grandmother Sarah, her dog Hank, her mother and father and she had been a victim of horrible child abuse for most of those years. Just when Sarah's home life seemed to finally be almost normal, and she felt loved again, that love was taken from her. Carol and John Peterman tried to console her, but even they could not understand why one child had to suffer so much. It wasn't fair. As Carol held Sarah and let her sob into her chest, Carol was devastated for her and knew Sarah's heart was broken beyond repair.

News traveled fast in a small town, and as the old red Ford pickup truck was pulled from the river, many of the townspeople watched and shook their heads in sadness and disbelief. Most of them stood on the banks of the Snake River to watch the ordeal. Ben Jackson sat in his car, on the highway above, and watched as Harvey's body was pulled from the old truck and placed in the coroner's van.

Chapter Nine

1929

Samantha Howard twirled in front of her full-length mirror. She was pleased with what she saw, although she knew her father would not be pleased at all. She was wearing the latest fashion, complete with beads down past her waist and the skirt high above her knees. Her father would call her a tart or say she was brazen. But, only if he saw her. Samantha didn't plan for him to see her tonight.

She tucked her long, blonde hair under the hat and cursed silently about its length. She wanted to cut it all off and wear it short like those girls they called "flappers", but she didn't dare. Cutting her hair would be a blatant act of defiance. And if she asked, she knew her father would never allow it. She knew she dare not defy him. It was enough that she wore these clothes and would sneak out of the house when her parents retired to their bedroom for the evening.

She heard the chimes of the grandfather clock in the parlor. It was eight o'clock. She had promised she would meet him at half past eight. She planned to leave soon and sneak out the back door by the maid's quarters. Pretending to have a headache, and asking to be excused from dinner, so she could go to bed early, had helped with her plan. Her parents would never suspect she would be anywhere other than her bed.

She was giddy with excitement and primped over and over in her mirror. She took a long look at herself and hoped he would be as pleased with her new clothes as she was. She was a tiny young girl with white blonde hair and big, blue eyes. She was sixteen years old, although she had told him she was eighteen.

"He doesn't need to know my real age." She said to herself as she gazed into the mirror. "Besides," she said with a sly smile, "Ladies don't tell their real age anyway."

She knew most ladies tried to appear younger than their real age, not older, but things were different for Samantha. She wanted to live her life differently than her mother and aunts. She wanted to really live, and live by her rules, not those of her family.

"The roaring twenties! What a great time to be alive." She said happily and with one last look in her mirror added, "Look out Alexander John Thomas! Here I come!"

She grabbed her long wool coat and slipped quietly out her bedroom door, down the long hall, to the staircase that led to the massive kitchen and out the back door. She took a deep breath of cool night air and breathed easy knowing she had managed to get out of the house without being seen. She pulled her coat tight to her chest and eased out through the main gate of the Howard Mansion that overlooked the Puget Sound and the bright lights of the city. It was the winter of 1929.

Samantha's father was one of the richest men in Seattle. He had made his fortune in the timber business, just after World War I, and he was a stern, hard man. No one crossed Benjamin Howard, for fear of his wrath, except one man. The one man was John Thomas. They were bitter enemies and fierce competitors. There was plenty of business for both Benjamin Howard and John Thomas in the lucrative timber business, but both men hated the other, and had tried to destroy each other for years.

So, when Samantha Howard, the only daughter of Benjamin Howard, met and fell in love with Alexander John Thomas, the only son of John Thomas, they knew they faced an uphill battle with their fathers.

As she hurried along the dark street, huddled into her coat, Samantha thought again about the dilemma.

"How will I ever tell my father about Alexander?" She sighed to herself.

She knew if her father found out his daughter was seeing the son of his enemy, he would forbid her to see him again. And Samantha knew she could not risk that. She had worried about it ever since she and Alexander met at the New Year's Eve party.

She had been playing around and acting silly, while practicing the Charleston with her girlfriend, when Alexander approached her. "I believe the dance was meant to be enjoyed by a man and woman." He teased and smiled at Samantha.

"Won't you allow me?" He said as he bowed at the waist and held out his hand.

She had been embarrassed that this handsome young man had witnessed her childish actions, blushed and held out her hand as an answer to his invitation. It took only one touch of his hand and one look at his handsome face, and Samantha knew she was in love. They danced, and it felt as though they had danced together all of their lives. Everything was so natural and easy for the couple, and even though they dance to every song, they both preferred the slow ones, in the dimly lit room, so they could hold each other close.

He introduced himself as Alexander and told her he was a student at Seattle University. Alexander and Sam spent the entire evening together and both felt they had found the magic of love they had heard and read about. As they walked out into the foyer, after the last dance, and into the bright lights for the first time, Samantha noticed a very distinct birthmark on his ear, but didn't comment on it. She wanted to get to know him better and didn't think it was appropriate to ask him about it.

Not wanting the evening to end, they sat together and talked for another hour or so. It never occurred to Samantha to ask his last name, nor did he ask hers, until it was time to go home.

"I would like to call on you, Samantha, but I just realized I don't even know your last name."

"Howard. It's Samantha Howard. What's your last name, Alexander?"

"Thomas." He replied slowly with a strange look on his face.

The Howard family had never formally met the Thomas family. But the fathers knew each other and both had informed their families of the feelings they had for one another. Once Alexander and Samantha shared their last names and discovered who they were, they were both stunned!

"I can't believe this." Alexander shook his head. "Your father is Benjamin Howard."

"And yours is John Thomas. Oh, Alexander, they hate each other. What are we going to do?"

"Look Sam," He said with determination, "I don't care who your father is and how our fathers feel about each other. I won't let you walk out of my life after such a wonderful night." Alexander held her in his arms. "We will think of some way to make everything work out. I promise you."

"Nothing can keep me from you now, Alexander." Sam replied softly. "No one needs to know about us for now."

So, for two months, Alexander and Samantha had stolen away whenever possible. They enlisted the help of their friends, as alibis when needed, and they spent every spare moment together. Sam knew her parents would be furious with her, not only for dating a man they would not approve of, but also for dating without a proper chaperone. In 1929, proper young ladies did not spend time with young men unless they were chaperoned, and Sam knew there was a good reason. She and Alexander spent hours kissing and caressing. It was becoming more and difficult not to let it go any further.

They avoided the painful subject of their families, but they both knew their love had reached a point of no return, and they would soon have to face the situation. They needed to decide how to approach their fathers and tell them that they were deeply and hopelessly in love.

Samantha reached the designated meeting place just as the rain started to fall. It was a bitterly cold night, and the rain turned to ice as it hit the ground. She shivered inside her coat and cursed herself for wearing the skimpy outfit on a night like this. She had planned to go to the dance again tonight and show off her new clothes, but when Alexander arrived he informed her of different plans.

"Sam, this is a perfect opportunity for us to be alone for as long as we want. A friend of mine is out of town and offered his place to us for the evening. It's on the edge of the city and very secluded. No one will know we are there."

Alexander was excited about the new plan and put his arms around her and kissed her cheek. The excitement was contagious as Sam returned his kiss, but on the lips this time.

"It sounds wonderful, Alexander. Let's go. I want us to be alone tonight." She said in a soft voice and gazed into his eyes.

As the car pulled away from the curb, Sam snuggled into his arm, and they both had the same thoughts. They knew tonight would be a very special night. And, it was.

Two months later, Samantha was miserable. She was violently ill with morning sickness, and she didn't need a doctor to tell her she was pregnant. She was terrified and knew their love affair could no longer be a secret. She was so tiny she knew the baby would start to show very soon, and she had to tell Alexander so they could work out their plans for the future. Maybe they would run away, far away from Seattle and the fathers that hated one another. Or maybe the fathers would learn to accept each other and settle their differences once they learned they would share a grandchild.

Sam had to talk to Alexander right away. She was so excited to tell him about the baby. She just knew he would be as thrilled as she was with the news. This baby would bring them together forever and they would be married and everything would be wonderful. Sam thought she had it all worked out.

It was the end of May, and Alexander was very involved with his final exams at the University. He would graduate in June and had very little time for Sam in the past month. Sam understood the pressures he faced before his graduation and knew everything would be all right once it was over. They had not had another time together since the night they borrowed the house from Alexander's friend. Sam couldn't believe she was pregnant after just one time. It has been her first and only time.

A friend of his father had offered Alexander a job with a top stock brokerage firm. All the wealthy people of Seattle were getting richer in the stock market, and Alexander and his father had invested heavily. Samantha didn't pay much attention to Alexander when he rambled on about the various stocks he purchased. She thought business was for men and she had no interest in the stock market. She didn't care about anything except Alexander, and now the baby, and their future together.

She knew time was running out fast and soon they would be forced to tell their families. But first she had to tell Alexander. She couldn't wait.

It took numerous messages to Alexander before he could respond to her and set a time to meet. He was under such pressure to do well on his finals that he hadn't had time for her and was irritated that she insisted he find the time to meet with her. Didn't she understand how difficult this time was for him? But, he finally managed to get away from his studies and arranged to meet her at the park near the pier. She immediately told him the exciting news, but Alexander didn't react with the enthusiasm Sam had envisioned.

"Samantha, how could this happen?" Alexander was in shock when she told him. "I thought we were careful!" He raised his voice this time and shouted at her.

"We only did it one time. There must be some mistake!" He paced the ground, clenched his fists and glared at Samantha. How can you be sure? Have you seen a doctor?"

"I'm sure Alex. I have morning sickness every day and I've missed my monthly. I'm sure."

"This is not good timing, Sam. Why did this happen now?"

Sam had expected him to be surprised but never expected him to be angry. She was stunned and deeply hurt by his reaction.

"I thought we were careful too, Alexander. I don't know why it happened now, but it did and we're going to have a baby."

She was so disappointed in him. She thought he would hold her and kiss her and tell her how much he loved her, but he didn't.

"What will we do, Alexander?" She asked as she put her face in her hands and wept.

She felt miserable. The morning sickness was there again, even though it was in the afternoon, and the reaction from Alexander made her feel even worse. Now she hoped he had an answer for her question.

"Sam, my father has set me up in business with his friend and loaned me a fortune to invest in the market. I can't let him down right now. He expects so much from me. My whole family expects so much from me."

Sam just sat watching him and listening to him. She started to realize this would not be easy for either one of them. They had tried to pretend no one else mattered, but the truth was, a lot of other people would be affected by what they had done. Alexander spoke softer now and had a sad look in his eyes.

"I'm sorry I yelled at you, Sam. It's such a shock and I have all these plans and all the pressure to do well on the finals. I'm just not prepared to handle something like this. Maybe in a couple of years, but not now."

"Alexander, I can't change what has happened. I just need to know that you will be with me and help me get through this."

"What do you mean, Sam? You mean you want to get married?"

"Well yes. What else is there to do? I just assumed we would be married. I thought we were in love!" She cried and put her arms around him.

"I do love you." He replied as he pulled her away from him and looked sadly into her eyes.

"But I can't get married to you or anyone right now. My father would disown me. I don't know what to do, really I don't. But I do know I can't be a father to your baby."

"This is our baby, not just mine." She pleaded, "Please Alexander, we can make this work. We will go to our families and tell them the truth. They will accept it in time. It will be okay, really it will."

She knew she was begging and realized she was getting nowhere. He looked frightened and almost as sick as she felt.

"I just don't know. I need time to think."

"Alex........." She reached for him again but he pushed away.

"Sam, please just give me time to think. I've got to go."

Sam watched him walk away and as he disappeared, she felt the morning sickness return. She put her head down, between her legs, until it passed. She felt so alone.

Chapter Ten

Sam managed to hide her pregnancy until the seventh month. One morning her mother walked in without knocking while Sam was undressed. She had known Sam was not feeling well and noticed she spent most of her time in her room instead of out with her friends. But, when she questioned Sam, she was told she decided to study every chance she could in preparation for college next year. Her mother assumed this was another phase she was going through and left her alone. Sam had been careful to choose clothes that did not show her figure and that had been easy with the new fashions that were loose and flowing that summer and fall.

When her mother saw Sam without her clothes that day she was completely shocked. She cried and carried on about how Sam's father would never forgive her. She was clearly afraid for Sam, but wanted to help her get through it. She tried to get Sam to talk about it, but she refused to tell anyone who the father was and only said, "You don't know him" which was partially true. She knew it was bad enough to be pregnant, but she felt certain her father would disown her if he knew the father of this baby.

Sam's mother finally settled down enough to think about the situation, and told Sam she would keep the secret as long as she could, but she wanted Sam to have proper medical attention and knew it would not be possible without telling her husband. Sam's father knew most of the doctors in the area, and she had no doubt all of them would refuse to hide the information from the powerful Benjamin Howard.

Ellen Howard decided the news would be best coming from her, and not from Sam, so she offered to tell her husband and hopefully protect her daughter from some of his initial reaction, which she knew would be outrageous.

"Benjamin, I must tell you something and I ask that you stay calm and discuss it with me."

Benjamin was distracted by worries from his office, and did not have patience with his wife.

"Just tell me and get it over with!" He said, still not giving much attention to his wife. Samantha's mother did not respond. She needed his full attention for this situation, and she waited for him to give it to her.

"What is it?" He questioned, and this time turned from his papers to look at his wife. The look on her face told him she had something very important to say, and he put the papers down on his desk and sighed. Tell me what's on your mind, Ellen."

She took a deep breath and sighed. "Samantha is pregnant."

Benjamin Howard was immediately furious. "How could that be?" He shouted, "She is just seventeen years old. She hasn't even been introduced into society!" He stormed back and forth.

"Who is the father? I'll kill him!"

"Benjamin, please calm down." Her mother pleaded. "Samantha refuses to tell me anything. She only cries, and tells me she just wants to die. I'm so worried about her and concerned for her health. I'm taking her to the doctor tomorrow."

"Her health be damned!" He screamed. "She has betrayed me and this family. How will we ever face this community and our friends knowing we have a tramp for a daughter?"

Benjamin Howard could not accept the fact that his only daughter had betrayed him. And, he had no tolerance for betrayal.

"Benjamin, she must see a doctor. She is in her seventh month and she needs medical care."

"You will keep her secluded in this house until the baby is born. Under no circumstances will she be allowed to leave. I will arrange for a doctor to come here. I want no one to know about this. Is that understood?"

"Yes, Benjamin."

As he turned to leave the room, he added with a look of hate,

"And when I find out the name of the father, I swear I will kill him!"

Sam's mother was torn between her daughter who needed her, and her husband who was angry and hurt. She knew the battle had just begun. During the next month, Samantha was confined to her room and was not allowed any company. Her friends and school was told she was very ill and contagious and not allowed to leave home. Sam was desperate to see Alexander, but there was no way to communicate with him.

Samantha was eight months pregnant when the stock market crashed on October 29, 1929. Even though Alexander had maintained some contact with Sam, he was too involved with his new job and the stock market to give her much time or attention. He refused to tell their families about their relationship, and forbid Sam to tell anyone, saying he couldn't jeopardize his business with his father just yet. And, he seemed different. He no longer looked at her the same way. It seemed he couldn't look at her at all, like he was almost embarrassed to be with her, and ashamed of how he felt.

Sam was devastated. She loved Alexander and couldn't understand his behavior since she had told him about the baby. On the few occasions they were able to meet, he didn't ask about the baby or how Sam was feeling. He was totally consumed by his own world of business and stocks and could talk of nothing else.

The front page of the Seattle Times brought a series of bad news. The stock market had crashed, and many of the local investors and business lost everything. Benjamin Howard had always thought investing in other men's companies was foolish, and he sat smugly at the long dining room table, reading of the devastation caused by the collapse of the market. His fortune was still intact, but many of his friends and business acquaintances had suffered greatly.

One man in particular had lost everything. The story of John Thomas, Alexander's father, was on the second page of the newspaper. It told the sad story of the wealthy businessman who had committed suicide the day after of the crash. His business and home had been mortgaged, and he had invested everything into the stock market with the intentions of becoming even richer. It never occurred to him that he could lose it all. His son, Alexander John Thomas, was said to be devastated and was trying to save the family business, but he too had lost heavily in the crash. Three days later, Alexander sent a note to Samantha.

> *My Dearest Sam,*
>   *Please forgive me for not being strong enough to*
> *stand by your side. I have failed you and our baby and*
> *now I have failed the Thomas family. Please know that*
> *I love you. I am not capable of handling the failures*
> *in my life now. Good bye, my love.*
>   *Alexander*

That same day the newspaper ran his picture on the front page with the caption, "Son Follows in Father's Footsteps, Another Thomas Suicide".

Sam collapsed after reading his note. When she opened her eyes, she was in terrible pain. The trauma of knowing Alexander was dead had caused her to go into an early labor. She was writhing in pain, and the doctor was preparing her for the delivery when her father entered the room. He stood at her bedside with the note from Alexander and the page from the newspaper in his hands.

"You have disgraced this family, Samantha." He said without emotion. "I will not have the bastard child of the Thomas family in my home."

Through her pain, Sam saw that he held the note and realized that he knew. The secret was out, but it didn't matter any more. Nothing mattered now that Alexander was dead. Her father continued to stare at her with a mixture of disappointment and hate.

"When this child is born, it will be taken from you and away from this house. You will never see it again."

He turned to walk from her room as the pain of labor tore through her seventeen-year-old body. Sam wanted to die.

Sam's mother and their maid, Virginia, helped the doctor with the delivery of the baby girl. She was almost a month premature, but everything was fine and the doctor told them she was as healthy as if she had gone full term. She was just a little smaller than normal, but that had been a blessing for her tiny, young mother. Ellen Howard cleaned and wrapped the newborn, all the while tears poured down her cheeks. She was heart broken for her daughter and her granddaughter. As she placed the tiny baby in Sam's arms, she said tearfully, "You must name her, Samantha. Before he takes her, please give her a name. You must always know her name!"

Sam held the little bundle and sobbed as she gazed into her eyes. Even though she was just born, she could already see the baby resembled her father and the tiny, perfect little face was trying its best to focus on Samantha. It was a moment that seemed to go into slow motion for Sam. She wanted to remember every detail of this child that would soon be taken from her and she inspected every inch of the newborn. She turned the baby's head to one side and let out a sob as she touched a tiny birthmark on her baby's ear. It was the same birthmark that Alexander had on his ear. The same birthmark that Sam had kissed and teased him about. And suddenly, she felt better. This birthmark would mean she would always be able to recognize her baby. And, then she knew. She would find her somehow.

As she stroked her baby's soft hair and kissed her tiny face, Sam looked up at her own heartbroken mother and replied, "Her name is Alexis."

Chapter Eleven

Now that she had been bathed and fed, Alexis was sleeping soundly. Samantha was physically and emotionally exhausted and felt numb from the pain of losing Alexander. Their baby had been born the day after he had died. Sam loved him so much, and now she saw Alexander in her newborn baby. Alexis had so many of his features and even had a small birthmark on her ear, just like her father. She thought it was such a miracle to have a healthy baby that looked so much like him. More tears fell as she realized her baby would never know her father, and she would never see him again.

Then, terror sat in as Sam recalled her father's angry words, "When this child is born, it will be taken from you."

"He can't possibly mean that." Sam consoled herself as she talked to her sleeping baby. "He will change his mind when he sees you, Alexis. How could he not love you?"

Sam stroked the tiny bit of hair on her baby's head and watched her sleep until exhaustion took over, and Sam could no longer keep her eyes open. She feel asleep with Alexis snuggled safely in her arms.

When she woke, Sam instantly knew something was wrong. Her baby was gone. She had been taken from her arms while she slept. She struggled to get out of bed and found she had very little strength and felt dizzy. She rang the bell on her nightstand, and Virginia came into the room.

"Oh, Samantha, you are awake. I'll get your father." Her maid and friend told her as she turned to leave the room.

"Wait, Virginia. Where is my baby?" Sam struggled to get up but found she couldn't. Her body felt drugged. "Please tell me. Where is Alexis?"

"Your father will be here soon, Samantha." Virginia said softly and did not meet Sam's eyes as she spoke. "Please stay in bed. You have been given medication to help you relax, and you shouldn't try to walk. I'll check in on you later."

Within moments after Virginia left the room, Samantha's father appeared. He had always been a hard man, but the look in his eyes, as he glared at Sam, frightened her.

"Samantha." He said sternly, "You are seventeen years old and you are still a minor child."

He stood erect with his hands folded across his chest. "I have made decisions that will be best for you and this family."

Once again Sam felt terror rush through her body as she waited for him to continue.

"Your clothes and personal items have been packed. You will leave tomorrow on the ship for London where you will finish your education. Virginia will go with you as your chaperone."

Sam was so stunned it took a minute for her foggy mind to process what he said. And, than it sunk in. She was being sent away from her home and family.

"Father, please don't do this!" She pleaded with him. "I'm sorry I have embarrassed you, but please don't send us away."

It occurred to Sam that he was sending them away to save the embarrassment to the family and he was going to let her keep her baby. If she had to leave home in order to keep Alexis, she would do it. She couldn't give up her baby! So, she conceded, thinking she could manage anything if only she could keep her.

"Please at least give me a few days to prepare, Father." I need some time to regain my strength and I'll need to make purchases before the trip. I have no clothes or nursery for my baby."

He never moved and his face showed no emotion as he said, "Samantha, you and Virginia will leave tomorrow as planned. Your baby will not go with you."

"No, Father! Nooooo!" She wailed and tried to get up from her bed. But her wobbly legs refused to hold her, and she collapsed to the floor as she tried to reach her father.

"Please Father, I beg you." She cried. "Please don't take my baby. Please don't take Alexis."

"I'm sorry Samantha, but I am doing what is best for you. Someday you will understand I have made the right decision. Your baby has already been taken away."

Samantha sobbed, uncontrollably as he picked her up and placed her back on the bed. As she sobbed into her pillow he opened the bedroom door and told Virginia to get the doctor.

"Tell him to give her another sedative to calm her down. And, have her ready to leave the house at eight o'clock in the morning. Your ship sails for London at noon."

Benjamin Howard turned and walked down the massive staircase as Virginia looked after him in disgust and asked herself, "What kind of man discards his daughter and granddaughter?"

But she knew what kind of man he was. She had worked for the Howard family for two years and knew he was very cold and selfish. He had the reputation of being ruthless in business, and she figured he had forgotten how to separate the business world from his family. The decision he made today was just another business decision in his mind. He had not given a thought to the feelings of his daughter or his wife.

Virginia's job at the Howard Mansion was to care for Mrs. Howard and Samantha, and she had learned to love them. She and Sam had become friends, and she didn't mind being sent to Europe with her, but she was so sorry for her. She knew Sam was devastated after Alexander had committed suicide, and now, she was losing her baby. It was so sad. She despised Benjamin Howard for his cold heart.

The sedative made Samantha sleep through the rest of the day and all night. Virginia woke her at six o'clock and helped her bathe and dress for the long voyage. Samantha was still weak from childbirth and didn't speak while preparations were made to leave. Breakfast went untouched and Virginia was worried about her young charge. She had asked the doctor for a supply of pills to help Sam relax. She knew her friend was facing a difficult future.

Sam was like a zombie, with no emotions, and her beautiful blue eyes were full of sorrow. Her parents were waiting in the foyer when Sam and Virginia came down the stairs, ready for departure.

Ellen Howard looked drained, and her eyes were swollen and red from the tears shed all night long. Benjamin Howard was stoic, and as he stood near the door waiting for her, Sam thought she saw a tiny tear in his eye. He quickly hugged her.

"Everything will be fine, Samantha. You'll see."

"Goodbye, Father." Sam said as she looked into his eyes. She searched them for any sign of emotion. She needed to know what kind of man could do what he had done to his own daughter. Sam would never forget his face as they parted. There was fleeting moment of tenderness and then he turned away. She realized he could not bear to look at her and see the pain he had caused his only daughter.

Benjamin Howard, ever the stern businessman, quickly regained his composure and gave last minute travel instructions to Virginia as Sam turned to her mother and hugged her tightly. She loved her mother, but knew she would never challenge her husband and his decisions, even for her own daughter.

"I'm so sorry, Samantha." She whispered into her ear as they held each other. "You will be safe with Virginia."

She pulled Sam from her, looked deep into her eyes and added, "You must try to put this all behind you, Sam. You are young and your whole life is ahead of you."

Her mother turned to the entry table behind her, picked up a wrapped package and handed it to Sam. "Please make use of this, Samantha. One day, you will be glad you did. Good-bye, Sweetheart. I love you."

She tried to remain composed but Sam saw the trembling and heard the cracking of her voice and knew this was very hard for her. She was losing her baby, too.

Sam kissed her cheek and said, "I love you too, Momma. Thank you for the gift. Goodbye."

Virginia helped Sam into the car and instructed the chauffer to drive them to the pier. They had a long journey ahead of them. Sam was still physically exhausted from childbirth and emotionally scarred from losing her baby, and the man she loved so deeply. She felt she had lost everything that mattered to her. She felt alone and empty as she stared out the window while the driver maneuvered through the morning traffic and the streets of Seattle.

Sam was so numb from the shock of what was happening, she had almost forgotten the gift her mother had placed in her hand. She stared at the package as more tears filled the corners of her eyes and slowly tore away the paper. It was a lovely leather-bound journal. Samantha Ellen Howard, 1929 was engraved in gold on the front cover. Her mother had written a note on the inside cover.

My Darling Samantha,
 Please remember we learn the most, and become stronger, because of the difficult times we face in our lives. You have suffered a great loss and my heart breaks because you are hurt. Try to put your thoughts into this journal and tell your story. Putting them on paper will help you heal. Time heals all wounds, even the very deepest of wounds. I will always love you more than life as I know you will always love Alexis.
 Your Loving Mother,
 Ellen Howard
 November 1929

Sam cried as she held the gift to her chest. Her mother knew how hard this was for her, and she understood how Sam felt. It helped ease the pain, just a little.

Virginia took care of the registration with the purser and helped Sam to their stateroom. Benjamin Howard had arranged for their passage and booked only the very best for them. They had a lovely suite with two bedrooms and a spacious living area. Virginia was excited as she inspected their home for the next several weeks, but Sam didn't see any of it. She simply went to her room and lay down to rest. She had been sent away from her home and family. She had lost Alexander, and her baby had been taken from her arms. Her whole life had been ripped away and she had never felt such loneliness and sorrow.

As she stared at the ceiling, and tears fell from her eyes, she heard the faint rumbling of the ship's engines and felt the ship start to move. She wanted to scream out, "Please don't take me away! Bring back Alexander and Alexis!"

Without the sedative to numb her mind, the reality of what had happened in the past two days sat in and Sam sobbed openly and uncontrollably. Virginia tried to comfort her, but nothing could console Sam. Virginia cradled the young woman in her arms and let her cry until there were no more tears. She finally convinced Sam to take another sedative and held her hand as she started to calm down and get sleepy. Before sleep consumed her, Samantha looked at her friend and spoke.

"Virginia, I'll find my baby! If it takes a life time, I swear I'll find Alexis."

"I hope you do, Sam. I really hope you do."

Chapter Twelve

Samantha and Virginia arrived at the Port of London three weeks later and were met at the pier by a tall, thin gentleman. Sam's father hired him to make all the arrangements for his daughter's transportation, housing and schooling while she was in Europe.

Samantha had no idea how long she was expected to stay in London, but knew her father would let her know when she would be allowed to return home. She only knew she was sent here to finish her schooling and to try and forget what had happened to her in the past few weeks. But she couldn't forget. She couldn't forget Alexis or Alexander. She couldn't stop thinking of them, and knew she would never forget.

"Welcome to London, Miss Howard." He said in a very formal manner and with a strong British accent. "My name is Henry Whittaker." He continued as Sam held out her hand, and he bent to kiss it lightly.

"Very nice to meet you, Mr. Whittaker. This is my traveling companion, Miss Virginia Ellis."

"How do you do, Miss Ellis?" He said as he turned to Virginia and also bent to kiss her hand.

"Fine, thank you." Virginia said as her voice quivered. Sam heard the quiver and knew her friend well enough to know she was nervous with the attention from the stranger. Sam also knew Virginia was somewhat shy and not comfortable around men.

"My driver will take us into the city where I have arranged for your housing. I hope everything meets with your approval."

He had their luggage delivered to the huge, strange looking vehicle and helped the two girls into the spacious back seat. He sat facing them in the other seat, and once they were on the road, he offered tea and biscuits from the built-in bar.

He had been instructed to do everything possible to make them feel at home and to spare no expense. Henry Whittaker had not met Mr. Howard from Seattle, but in the weeks it took for Samantha to arrive, her father sent daily telegrams with detailed instructions as to how his daughter and her companion should be cared for.

Sam's first impression of England was how much it looked like the state of Washington. The English countryside had similarities to that of Seattle, with the rolling hills and heavy humidity hanging in the air. It was drizzling rain and everything was very green from all the moisture, just like home. But the similarities ended there. The cars drove on the wrong side of the street, the houses and buildings were old and the people talked so funny.

Sam had a hard time understanding Mr. Whittaker as he tried to point out things of interest to the two Americans. She knew he spoke English but this was a real different type of English to her.

"If you are not too weary from the journey, I would like to show you some of the city. When you get settled, you'll want to take in all the sights of London, but for now you must at least see a few of my favorites. We will be passing Trafalgar Square, the Westminster Abbey and Big Ben just to name a few." He continued as the limousine drove toward London. "Would you indulge me while I attempt to give an amateur guided tour?"

Virginia looked to Sam with raised eyebrows, wanting Sam's permission to continue with the tour. "That sounds wonderful, Mr. Whittaker. We would like that very much, wouldn't we, Virginia?"

"Oh yes!" Virginia said a little to quickly. "I mean, we would enjoy seeing some of the city, Mr. Whittaker."

The sights of the foreign city fascinated Virginia. She questioned the gentleman every chance she could and held onto every word. Samantha noticed Virginia's excessive talking was a little out of character, but thought it must be the excitement of being in a new place.

Samantha tried to feel the excitement of being in a foreign country too, but her heart just wouldn't let her. She had fought tears and depression for weeks now. The medication she had taken at the beginning of the trip had helped relax her, but she didn't want to rely on the medication any longer and was determined to get through this difficult period of her life without it. There was nothing she could do now, but make the best of the situation her father had put her in.

Virginia and Mr. Whittaker continued to chat as the chauffer drove into the city. "We have just crossed the Thames River, and we are now passing the Tower of London. Originally the Tower of London was outside the city walls. This tower has served as a royal residence and a state prison. It covers approximately thirteen acres. We are presently at the east-end of the city."

Upon entering London, the Americans immediately noticed the busy city streets, with red double-decker buses, full of people. The girls were busy turning their heads from one side of the street to the other, taking it all in, while Mr. Whittaker described the historical sights.

"We are now in the center of London and this is known as Charing Cross. You will see the railroad station to your left and to your right is the famous Trafalgar Square, which was constructed for England's greatest naval hero, Admiral Nelson. He is buried in a tomb in the crypt beneath St Paul's Cathedral, which we will see later on the tour."

"You really bury people under churches, Mr. Whittaker?" Virginia asked with a worried look on her face.

"Yes, Miss Ellis. In fact it is quite an honor for the deceased and customary in many European countries."

"Oh, I'm sure it is, Mr. Whittaker. I've just never heard of it before. I guess there is nothing wrong with it." Virginia mumbled and turned toward the window.

"You will notice we are now on the Strand Avenue. This famous street runs from Charing Cross to the original City of London following the Thames River."

Even with all the sadness Samantha felt inside, she started to enjoy the sights and surprised herself by asking questions right along with Virginia.

"Is this really where the Queen of England lives?" Sam asked as they approached Buckingham Palace. "I would love to see the inside. I'll bet it's lovely."

"Yes, Miss Howard. Buckingham Palace is the official residence of the royal family and has approximately 40 acres of land behind those walls. But, I'm afraid it is off limits to visitors."

"Oh look, Sam! It's Big Ben!" Virginia spotted the huge tower as they turned the corner.

"Yes, ladies. We are at the north end of Parliament and this is called the Clock Tower. It is famous for the great bell that was the work of Sir Benjamin Hall, thus the name of Big Ben. It is 320 feet high. Just ahead you will see the Westminster Abbey and Parliament Square. This Gothic structure was started in the eleventh century. Some of the kings and queens of England are buried there."

With the urging of Samantha and Virginia, Mr. Whittaker instructed the chauffer to expand the tour of the city. And two hours later, they had driven by St Paul's Cathedral, the Tower Bridge, the Bank of England, the National Gallery, Tate Gallery and the Victoria and Albert Museum.

"When you have settled in, you will want to take some time to see inside the galleries and museums. We have some of the best in the world here in London."

"I would like that very much." Sam replied. "The tour has been very interesting, Mr. Whittaker. Thank you very much. I never realized there would be so much to see in London." Sam said with enthusiasm. She realized she was actually seeing some of the famous places she read about in the history books. It fascinated her, and she felt herself smile for the first time in a long time.

"Oh, I am afraid you've only just began to see the city. I will be happy to show you more."

"I can't wait!" Virginia replied as she smiled at him.

Sam caught the smile Virginia had given him, and thought she noticed she had been acting strange around Mr. Whittaker. Virginia was twenty-four years old and always claimed she planned to be an old maid. She was very quiet and reserved and spent her spare time reading books or sewing in her room, never showing any interest in men. But today Sam saw a different side of Virginia. This Virginia was giddy, and it occurred to Sam that she was flirting with Henry Whittaker.

He was very well dressed and even though he was not a handsome man, he was very polite and charming. He looked to be about thirty years old, yet his hair was already thinning. Sam noticed he gazed at Virginia just a little longer than necessary, and realized Virginia and Mr. Whittaker were drawn to one another. It made her smile as she looked out the window and pretended not to notice the mating game between her friend and this English gentleman.

The apartment was in the west-end of London in Westminster on Victoria Street. It was within walking distance to the private school where Samantha would continue her education. The buildings were stone or brick, and every yard had a garden. The building was three stories high, but Sam's apartment was on the first level with a lovely view of the neighborhood park.

Mr. Whittaker had taken care of everything. The kitchen was stocked with food and beverages, including boxes of English tea. The attractive two bedroom flat had been furnished with comfortable furniture and linens. Even though it was small and old, it was clean and cozy with a fireplace in one corner and a small garden off the dining room. And in the other corner of the living room, surrounded by windows, stood an easel and a small wooden table covered with canvas and paints. Samantha loved it. Everything was lovely, and she immediately felt she belonged there.

"This is perfect, Mr. Whittaker! But how did you know I loved to paint?" She was curious because even though she knew her father had made the arrangements for her, he did not know she had a passion for painting and had never discussed it with her. He had always been too busy with his work to know anything about Samantha's hobbies.

"I received a long letter from your mother with specific instructions on everything, including your favorite foods, colors and styles. She told me you enjoyed painting in your spare time, and asked that I make sure you had the necessary supplies. I hope you'll find everything you need, Miss Howard."

"Thank you so much for all your efforts, Mr. Whittaker. The apartment is lovely."

"Samantha, it is called a flat in England." Virginia chimed in, now with a touch of a British accent. "Isn't that right, Mr. Whittaker?"

"As a matter of fact it is, Miss Ellis." He grinned at her attempt to use the accent while correcting Sam.

"Won't you please call me Virginia, Mr. Whittaker?"

"Thank you, Virginia, I will. And please call me Henry."

Sam watched as the two flirted again and was pleased to see Virginia so enthralled with a gentleman. She remembered those feelings of giddiness when she first met Alexander and had to stop herself from thinking about him again. She couldn't let herself do that right now. If she did, everything would be a reminder of what she had lost so recently. She forced herself to stay focused on this pleasant moment for Virginia. Virginia had been a wonderful friend, especially during these past few weeks and she deserved happiness.

Henry stood in the foyer of the flat, preparing to leave and hesitated as he opened the door. "Would you ladies join me for dinner this evening? I will give you a couple of hours to rest and ring for you at six o'clock, if you agree."

Samantha saw Virginia's eyes light up and knew that even though she was tired from the journey and the tour, she couldn't let her friend down. "We would be delighted to join you for dinner. We will see you at six o'clock, Mr. Whittaker."

"Smashing. And please dress casual. I want you to experience an authentic English dinner in the local pub. Oh, and Miss Howard, please call me Henry." He turned to leave and seemed to walk on air. Sam noticed his formal manner had become a little more casual.

As she closed the door she turned to Virginia and teased, "I have a funny feeling we might see quite a bit of Henry, don't you, Virginia?"

"Isn't he dreamy Sam, and so well mannered. I've never met an Englishman before. He is so formal. Don't you just love his accent, Sam?" Virginia rambled on while Sam nodded and grinned at her friend.

"Thank you for agreeing to have dinner with him, Sam. I was hoping he would ask to see me again, but I knew he was too much of a gentleman to ask right away. This is perfect, you know, having dinner with the three of us, like it's his job or something. Oh, Sam, I'm sorry, I didn't mean it that way. I just mean I am happy we can have dinner with him, you know so we can learn more about the food and customs for the area."

"Virginia," Sam laughed, "Settle down before you wear out. I have never seen you talk so much. You are making me tired just listening to you."

"I know, Sam. It's just that I have never met any one like him and I feel like I'm fourteen years old again. It's silly, isn't it? Oh, I hope I didn't seem foolish to him. Did I seem foolish, Sam?"

"No, Virginia, you didn't. You talked a lot, but you didn't seem foolish." Sam continued to tease her. "Actually, I think Henry enjoyed every minute of it."

"You really think so, Sam?"

"I really think so." Sam put her arms around her and hugged her. "Welcome to England, Virginia. I am so glad you came with me. Now, we had better get some rest before dinner."

Chapter Thirteen

Henry arrived promptly at six o'clock, and Sam and Virginia were ready to go. They wore simple wool skirts and sweaters knowing the wool would help fight off the chilly night air.

"I see you already know the importance of wool in the London climate." Henry remarked. "And I must say I have never seen wool worn more beautifully by two young ladies."

Virginia blushed as Sam grinned and said, "Oh, Henry, you are a charmer. But, don't forget we are from Seattle where the winter chill goes right through you. Wool has always been a big part of our winter wardrobe."

"Of course. I suppose there are some similarities between England and your part of the United States. The only part I'm a familiar with is Hollywood, California. But I am anxious for you to tell me all about Seattle."

"I'll be happy too, Henry." Virginia chimed in. "But right now, I'm famished. Let's eat before I die of hunger."

"I'm a bit hungry myself and can't wait to show you the pub. It is just a short walk from here. I hope you don't mind walking."

"Not at all, Henry." Sam replied. "The walk will do us good. I still feel like I'm swaying from all that time on the ship. It feels good to be on land, doesn't it, Virginia?"

"It sure does. I'm ready if you are." Virginia said as she reached for their coats and headed for the door.

The three new friends arrived at the Ale House at six thirty, and it was already crowded. The smell of cigars and beer was strong as they passed through the first part of the pub and made their way to the back section where the food was served. It was noisy and most of the people seemed to be in their twenties or thirties, laughing, telling jokes, playing Draughts or throwing darts while they made wagers on their abilities.

Sam immediately liked the atmosphere, and even though she knew she was younger than the group, she felt a part of it. She was totally content to watch the activities around her while Virginia and Henry were content to watch each other.

Sam picked up the menu and chuckled as she saw the list of offered food. Steak and Kidney Pie, Bangers and Mash, Fried Welsh Rarebit.

"Okay Henry, I know this menu is in English, but I have no idea what these dishes are. Would you mind ordering for me?"

"Yes please, for me too." Virginia laughed. "I'm afraid to place an order on my own. Heaven only knows what I would get."

"I'd be happy to order for both of you. The Ale House is famous for its Fish and Chips. Perhaps, that would be the best choice for your first English dinner."

And, he was right. The girls loved the English version of Fish and Chips and ate every bite. They laughed and exchanged stories for more than three hours that evening and by the time they walked back to the flat, Samantha, Virginia and Henry had become good friends.

During the next several months, Samantha and Virginia fell into a nice routine. Samantha attended classes at the private school just three blocks from their flat while Virginia tended to the cooking, shopping and cleaning. Samantha spent her evenings studying, painting or writing in the journal her mother had given her, while Virginia spent time with Henry.

Her mother had been right. The writing was good therapy, and she had written everything she could remember of the past year, starting with the first evening she met Alexander. As she wrote each evening, the memories came rushing back, and she re-lived each one of them. At times she cried as she wrote, but many times she laughed at the memories of the fun and wonderful times with him.

It made her realize that he had been too young and immature to handle what had been given him. She had no doubt that he loved her, but he was weak and afraid of his father, just as Sam had been afraid of hers. She was forced to face the mistakes they had made, and found herself wishing she could turn back the clock to do things differently. If she could, she would still be in Seattle. She would be with Alexander and their baby. If only she could turn back time.

The hardest part of the writing came when she wrote about Alexander's death and giving birth to Alexis, only to have her father take her away. As hard as it was to re-live those days, she knew she had to do it. She had to deal with the pain, so it would eventually go away. When her writing caused too much pain, she turned to her painting. Many hours were spent it front of the easel, painting furiously, while tears fell.

Every month got easier. Even though she still thought of Alexander and Alexis every day, she was finally able to think of them and smile with the memories. Her mind's eye pictured Alexander's handsome smile. And, the birthmark on Alexis' tiny ear, just like her father's, was the reminder that Alexis was definitely her father's daughter. Sam decided to focus on the good memories and put the bad ones to the back of her mind. She knew they would never go away completely, but would eventually fade a little.

On the day of Alexis's first birthday, Sam could not be consoled. She cried all day and prayed that Alexis was safe and with a good family. She talked to Alexis as though she were there with her and promised that she would find her some day. As therapy, Sam painted a portrait of a little girl who looked to be about one year old and hung it on her bedroom wall. She did not realize, at the time, that she had started an annual ritual. But, over the years, Sam painted a special portrait each year to celebrate and represent the birthday of her daughter. The facial features were from the imagination of the painter, for Sam could only imagine what her daughter looked like. Each portrait showed the tiny birthmark and the blue eyes, and in the corner of each painting, Sam added "Alexis, November 3rd".

Samantha finished her required education the following year, but had no desire to return to the United States just yet. She had taken all of the art classes offered at the English school, and each attempt at painting was better than her last. Virginia and Henry were her biggest fans and encouraged her to sell her work, but Sam scoffed at the idea that anyone would actually pay money for it. Instead, the walls of her flat were covered with her paintings of English gardens and landscape.

Samantha, Henry, and Virginia celebrated Sam's birthday that second summer by taking a trip to the countryside. Bath, England, was located just two hours from London by train and was famous for the natural hot springs built by the Romans long ago. The town was named for the Roman Baths that were thought to heal the sick, and people came from miles around to bathe in the warm water. It was a lovely day and the three enjoyed the rare English sunshine as they took in the sights of the quaint village.

When they stopped for lunch at a lovely outdoor café, Henry ordered a bottle of champagne, and Sam thought he was really going all out for her birthday. But when the bottle arrived and the glasses were filled, Henry made an announcement that Sam was not surprised to hear.

"Samantha, Virginia and I would like to wish you a very happy birthday!" He held his glass high and continued, "To our very dear friend, may you have many more and........." He hesitated just a moment, looked at Virginia, picked up her hand and kissed it. "And we would like for you to be the first to know."

Samantha looked at Henry and then Virginia, saw the grin on their faces, and knew before he said the words, "Virginia and I are going to be married."

"Oh my goodness, Henry! And Virginia, why didn't you tell me!" Sam exclaimed as she jumped up from her chair and hugged them both. "Congratulations! I'm so happy for you! When is the date?"

"We are hoping right away Sam, but of course I need to give a proper notice to your father and take care of the paperwork to allow me to stay in England as Mrs. Whittaker." Virginia gazed into Henry's eyes; he leaned over to kiss her cheek.

"Don't worry about giving notice to my father. I hardly need a chaperone any more, now that I'm nineteen years old. We will simply write to him and tell him you have received a better offer."

The three laughed, and Sam raised her glass to toast the couple, "To my very best friends. May you have all the happiness the world has to give."

"Thank you, Sam. I will miss you so much. Maybe we can find a flat close by. Henry's tiny place can't accommodate both of us so we will need to find another one before the wedding."

"I have a better idea, Virginia." Sam said thoughtfully. "Why don't you and Henry take our flat? The location is perfect, and it has plenty of room for two."

"I don't understand, Sam. Are you thinking of going back to Seattle? I thought you liked it here."

"Oh, I do. I love England. But I've been thinking about it for several months now, and if my father will agree, I want to go to Paris. I want to continue my art studies, and Paris is the place to be if you are a young, starving artist."

"Well, I doubt you will starve," Henry teased, knowing Sam's father sent an allowance each month. "But I agree that would be the perfect place for you to pursue your work. Here's to Sam and her pursuit of painting." He raised his glass as Sam and Virginia followed. "Just don't forget your friends when you become a famous artist, Sam."

"I'm not the kind of person who forgets the ones I love, Henry. Now, lets forget about me and get back to the two of you. We've got a wedding to plan."

Chapter Fourteen

Virginia and Henry were married and moved into the flat while Sam packed her things to prepare for the move to Paris. She took only the painting of Alexis, sent a couple of her favorites back to Seattle and left the rest hanging on the walls. Her father and mother were hesitant at first about Sam's plan to continue her studies, but after seeing her paintings they were convinced that this was the best thing for her. Sam's father was so impressed with her work that he offered to arrange for her care once again and hire another chaperone for her in Paris.

But Sam insisted she did not need a chaperone and had already made arrangements to stay with a fellow artist she had met in school. Janette was from Paris and had a small apartment in the Latin Quarter. She told Sam it was the perfect place for an artist, close to the University and the Seine River where the local artists painted and displayed their works.

So, in the fall of 1931, Mr. and Mrs. Henry Whittaker escorted Sam to the train station at Trafalgar Square where she would take the train to Dover, and then cross the English Channel. As she hugged her friends goodbye, Sam had mixed emotions. Virginia and Henry had been her family for nearly two years and she would miss them terribly. They were like a brother and sister to her, and both had helped her through a very difficult time in her life. But they all had their new lives ahead of them now, and it was time to move on. So, goodbyes were said, and promises were made to keep in touch.

As Sam boarded the ferry at Dover, she felt a new sensation. It was one of independence and freedom. She was finally on her own and pursuing a dream. She felt her heartbeat rush as she took a deep breath of the cool sea air. As the ferry pushed away from the pier, she watched the White Cliffs of Dover fade into the distance. Soon she would arrive in Calais, France. Just a few hours on the train would put her in Paris. She couldn't wait.

The next two years flew by. Sam loved being in Paris. The city was full of excitement. The restaurants were wonderful, the culture was fascinating and the scenery was lovely. The land surrounding the city was green and beautiful with gentle rolling hills. The climate was perfect with mild summers and cool winters. She spent many hours walking along the Seine or sitting at the outdoor cafes drinking café au lait and eating croissants with marmalade.

She took classes at the University and learned to speak enough French, so she could get buy without feeling foolish. She learned a great deal from the other artists and spent all of her spare time at the art galleries and museums. She became an expert, could name every famous artist, and when their work had been done.

Even though she continued to paint, and knew her paintings were good, she knew they would never be great. But that was okay. She loved being around the works of other artists almost as much as she loved to paint. And she enjoyed painting for herself. Her bedroom now had four paintings of little girls with the same birthmark on their ears and they comforted her as she said goodnight to their smiling faces each night.

Samantha was twenty-two years old when Ellen Howard sent a telegram and insisted she wanted to come to Paris and visit Samantha. Sam's mother had written letters every week since they were separated by the tragic events, and those letters had been a great source of comfort to Sam. It was the family connection Sam needed and made it easier for her to remain in Europe.

Sam had her own apartment by this time and enjoyed having her mother's company. Now that Sam was a grown woman herself, she learned about her mother, as a woman, and liked what she learned. She was a gentle, loving woman who was devoted to her husband, despite his many faults, and deeply loved her daughter. They had two wonderful months together, and Sam proudly showed off her knowledge of France and its language. It was fun getting to know one another once again, and it made Sam realize how much she missed her home.

So, when Ellen Howard gave Sam the idea of an art gallery in Seattle, Sam was immediately interested.

"Samantha, Seattle is the perfect place to open a gallery. With your connections in Paris and your eye for great talent, you could have the most impressive gallery in the city."

Her mother had an interesting idea, even if it was a little selfish. She knew her mother missed her and wanted her to move back to home. And, Sam knew she could not stay in Europe forever, now that her education was finished. It was time for her to get on with her life. This was the way to make it happen for both of them.

"Sam, you can have anything you need to get started. We will be partners. I will front the initial investment to open the gallery, and then it will be yours. You will make all the other decisions. It will be perfect for you. You can still paint and stay involved with the art world, and best of all you will be back home with me. Won't you think about it, Dear?"

And the following summer, Sam and Ellen Howard cut the ribbon at the grand opening of the Alexis Gallery. It was a huge success and was soon known as the best gallery in the Northwest. Samantha loved it and spent every spare minute working on it. She arranged to have an apartment built above the gallery, with a studio for her painting and huge windows overlooking the Puget Sound. It was perfect and Sam was happy with her life. There was only one thing missing. Alexis. She was five years old now. Sam imagined her with long, light brown hair and blue eyes, with her father's smile.

That was the year Sam started her search for Alexis. She managed to live on the money she made at the gallery, but that didn't leave much for the cost of the private detectives, so she was limited in her search. She knew she could never go to her father to request money. He had made it clear that she should be on her own financially, now that she was finished with her education and had been set up in her own business. Sam's mother had provided help to get the business started using the family money, but it was up to Sam to earn her own living. Her part of the family fortune had been placed in a trust fund and could not be touched until she was 40 years old. Benjamin Howard was adamant that a young person should earn their way in life.

Sam struggled for years to have enough money to hire private detectives. But the kind of detectives she could afford was not the best and never seemed to have any luck finding Alexis. It was a difficult task, locating a child that was taken so long ago. Sam held on to the hope that her name had remained the same.

Sam was a beautiful young woman and the eligible men of Seattle tried to win her over, but Sam had no interest in men. Her heart belonged to Alexander and once it was broken, it could not be mended. She never married and never regretted being alone. She had her art gallery and her dream of finding her daughter one day. Her life was full.

The years passed and time and again, Sam received bills for the work of various private detectives, always with the same results. They had come to a dead end or Alexis seemed to have dropped off the face of the earth. And, one insensitive investigator even suggested Alexis might not be alive. Several of them advised Sam to stop wasting her money, but Sam refused to give up. Alexis was a grown woman now, and it was too late for Sam to be a real mother to her, but she still wanted her daughter to know she had been loved and searched for all those years.

When Sam celebrated her fortieth birthday, and received the money from the family trust, her private art studio had 23 paintings of young girls with the tiny birthmark. Now, with no limit on what she could spend for private investigators, Sam pursued the search with a vengeance. She was more determined than ever to find her baby girl. She had made a promise all those years ago and she intended to keep it. So, hiring the very best detective she could find, the search for Alexis continued.

Chapter Fifteen

1959

Samantha sat at the back of the old church for the second time in less than six months. The church was full this time, and Sam thought she recognized a few of the faces from her last visit. She had never met Harvey Taylor, but knew she had to attend his funeral. After all, Harvey had married her daughter, and he was the father to her only grandchild. Her heart ached for the daughter she never knew and granddaughter she wanted to know. The poor child had lost her mother and father within just a few months. Sam wanted to run to her and hold her tight, but she knew she could not. Her mind wandered back to the conversation just last summer with Alexis, and she cried to herself remembering the unhappy results.

"Hello, Taylor residence." Alexis had answered the phone.

Silence.

"Hello." Alexis snapped this time. "Who is this?"

"Please." Samantha said softly with hesitation. "Please don't hang up."

"Who is this?" Alexis asked again with irritation.

"Am I speaking to Alexis Taylor?"

"Yes. Who wants to know?"

More silence.

Samantha lost her nerve and suddenly didn't know what to say. All those years of practicing what she would say to her daughter seemed lost now that she actually heard her voice. She tried to compose herself as her tears spilled from her eyes. Twenty-nine years was a long time but she never forgot the feeling of the soft skin and scent of her newborn baby so long ago. A mother never forgets.

"Alexis." She spoke the words slowly and carefully. "My name is Samantha Howard."

There was more silence while Alexis stiffened and waited for her to go on. Samantha took another deep breath to gather her nerve.

"Alexis, I am your mother."

"I know who you are." Alexis replied without emotion. "I got your letter."

"I had hoped you would respond to my letter. It's been over a month since I mailed it. I was afraid you hadn't received it."

Alexis did not reply.

"I would like to meet you, Alexis." Samantha said hopefully. I understand you have a daughter. I would like to see her."

"How did you find me?" Alexis snapped at her.

"I hired a private detective. It has taken many years to find you. Please, may I meet you? I can be there by tomorrow if I leave right away."

Alexis hesitated for a moment and felt a surge of excitement just before the anger sat in.

"What's the use? You are no mother to me. You didn't want me twenty-nine years ago, and now I don't want you. Don't ever contact me again."

As the telephone line went dead, Samantha caught a sob in her throat. How could she have handled this differently? Maybe she called too soon after sending the letter that explained who she was. She thought Alexis needed some time to adjust to having a mother in her life. So, Sam had waited almost a month before she called her. She had hoped Alexis would call her, so she had included her telephone number and address with the letter. But the call never came.

Alexis wanted no part of a reunion. She was stubborn, and even though she longed to meet the mother she had never known, her pride wouldn't let her. Alexis couldn't possibly know she had inherited her stubbornness and cold heart from the grandfather that sent her away when she was born. But, Samantha knew. She heard it in her voice that day. It was as though she was talking to the female version of Benjamin Howard. Sam would give her some time. She hoped Alexis would accept it someday and contact her. Sam had waited a long time, and she would wait longer for the right time to meet her daughter and family.

But Samantha never had the chance to meet her daughter. Instead, she attended her funeral less than one month after that telephone conversation.

Now, she sat at the funeral service of Alexis' husband and the tears poured down her face. She had spent all those years searching, and now she had lost her forever. Alexis had killed herself just as her father, Alexander, and grandfather, John Thomas. It seemed she had inherited the weakness of the Thomas family and the stubbornness of the Howard family.

Samantha's thoughts drifted back. For the thousandth time she asked herself why she and Alexander had not faced their families together all those years ago. They should have been married and raised their daughter together. He should have been strong enough to handle the financial loss from the crash of the stock market. And she should have been strong enough to stand up to her father and not let him take her baby. Her life had been full of regrets because of choices she had made when she was just a young girl. Oh, how she wished she could have back those days when she first met Alexander. If only she could, she would make better choices.

Now, here she was attending a second funeral. Why hadn't she insisted on seeing Alexis that day? Maybe she could have done something to prevent her suicide. Maybe she should have sent another letter to explain how her father had taken her away. Maybe she could have gotten to know her granddaughter so she could comfort her now that she was an orphan. But Samantha was a stranger to the sad little girl sitting in the front row. And this little girl did not need a stranger in her life right now. Instead, she needed the love and support of people she knew and loved, like the couple sitting next to her. Samantha would return to Seattle and make arrangements for Sarah to come live with her. She would come for her as soon as she could. She had to do everything just right.

Sam waited for the services to end and watched as the casket was wheeled out the door with little Sarah walking close behind. She was such a beautiful child even in her worn shoes and faded dress. Sam thought she looked so sad and lonely, and wanted to hold her, comfort her, and tell her she was not alone, and that she had a grandmother. But it was too soon. She knew Sarah had too much to deal with right now. She knew she had to take things slowly with her granddaughter.

She watched as the handsome couple walked with Sarah to the car and the young woman gathered Sarah into her arms. She helped her into the front seat of the car, next to her, and they drove away. Samantha didn't know the identity of this man and woman who had taken charge of Sarah, but she would contact the private detective and get the information she wanted. She needed more answers before making contact with this lovely little girl who looked so much like her.

It was a long drive back to Seattle and the roads were treacherous through the Blue Mountains this time of year. She should have brought Franklin, her chauffer, but she had wanted to be alone this trip. She enjoyed the drive and needed time alone to think about the turn of events. Besides, no one knew the real reason for her trip to Idaho again. Her father thought she was visiting an old friend that had moved to Boise. She couldn't take the chance that Franklin would mention a funeral or find out about Alexis, Harvey and Sarah. She would tell her father when the time was right. She had so many plans to work through now. She had already called her attorney to let him know about Sarah.

Sarah, Samantha, and her father were the only heirs to the Howard fortune. Sam's father was past seventy years old now and recently had taken less interest in the family business affairs and had asked Sam to assume many of the responsibilities. He still had no idea his only granddaughter had died and left him a great-granddaughter. Sam had so much to tell him once she got back home.

Sam turned on the wipers as she drove through the spitting snow. She hoped it would continue to melt as it hit the ground. She had never driven on snowy roads before and felt uneasy at the prospect. Seattle had lots of rain, but very seldom had snow and, of course, her chauffer usually drove everywhere she needed to go. She adjusted the heater in the car and put on her wool gloves as she felt the chill coming in through the windows. It was cold outside, and the car windows were frosting over.

The Mercedes started to climb the road leading into the Blue Mountains and passed a sign recommending chains for the road ahead.

Sam's mind was too busy to pay attention to the road signs. She had Sarah to think about now. She wanted to bring her to Seattle to live with her. She would send her to the best schools and hire the best tutors and teachers for her. She would take her on trips to Europe and cruises to the islands. She couldn't wait!

She tried to find a radio station, but the high mountain range drowned out any hope for reception. So, she let her mind wonder and reminisced about what had led her to this point in her life.

She had gone to great lengths to keep her search for Alexis a secret. Her father would disown her if he knew she had tried to locate the child he had taken from her and hidden so well. He almost accomplished his goal. Sam searched for years and the costs of the private detectives had been very expensive. But once she started to receive the funds from the family trust, she hired only the very best to try to find Alexis. But without the help of her mother, she doubted even the best would have picked up the old trail of the missing child.

Sam smiled as she thought how upset her father would be if he knew his money had gone to search for the granddaughter of his old enemy. He had managed to bribe and pay off attorneys and foster homes until there had been no trail to follow. The only clue she had was the first name of the baby and her date of birth.

Samantha secretly thanked her mother many times for advising her to give the baby a name when she was born. It gave Sam a connection to Alexis somehow, seeing her and calling her by her name, before she was taken from her. She never stopped thinking about her or searching for her.

Sam's thoughts moved on to her mother just then, and she thought about how much she loved her and missed her. Sam had moved back into the Howard Mansion when her mother became ill, so she could help take care of her. She kept her apartment over the gallery just as she left it and stopped in from time to time to paint without being disturbed. She still had all of the paintings of Alexis she had painted over the years and the walls were covered with them.

Sam knew her mother had never crossed her husband during their married life, but as Ellen Howard lay on her deathbed, she had called Samantha to her.

"I have loved your father all these years but I've never forgiven him for what he did to you. And, I have never forgiven myself for not trying to stop him from taking your baby."

"It's okay, Momma." Samantha replied as she held her frail hand. "That was a long time ago. We can't change the past."

"No, we can't. But maybe we can try to make up for it."

"What do you mean?"

"Samantha, I know you have been searching for her. I've known it for a long time.

Sam was surprised to hear her mother speak about the subject that had been taboo from the day Alexis was born. "How did you know, Momma?"

"A mother knows these things. I would have done the same. I can't imagine not having you in my life. You have been a wonderful daughter. I know you've had a broken heart, and I've watched you suffer all these years. There was nothing I could do until now."

Her mother continued as Sam sat full of curiosity. "I found some papers, Sam. They had been in the safe at his office all these years. When he retired last month, his assistant brought the boxes from his office here. So, while he was out of town for a few days, I knew I had to search and try to find something that would help you."

Sam was so excited she almost screamed. "Oh Momma! What did you find? Do you know where she is?"

"The day he took your baby, I told him you had given her the name Alexis and I told him to make sure her name was given to her caregiver. He was hesitant at first, but I insisted the baby have the name her mother had given her, and he finally agreed. The papers I found last month had her given name of Alexis. He did as I asked him to do. He didn't change the name you gave her, Sam. The attorney that handled the transfer of the child was from Boise, Idaho. It's all written down here. It will still be hard to find her, but it's a start."

She took a folded paper from the nightstand and gave it to Sam. "I'm so sorry things had to be this way, Sam. I hope you can forgive me."

"Oh Momma, thank you so much!" Sam cried as she hugged her frail mother. "I've never blamed you. I just wish things could have been different for all of us. I wish you could have known your granddaughter."

"Me too, Sam. Me too. Now, you go find Alexis."

"I will, Momma. I love you!"

"I love you too, Samantha."

Her mother died two days later. The following week, Sam was on her way to Idaho. That had been just over one year ago. Six months later, the private investigator located Alexis Taylor in Benton, Idaho. And, medical records showed this Alexis Taylor had a tiny birthmark on her ear. Sam had finally found her baby.

Samantha had written the letter to explain who she was and asked for Alexis to meet with her. She fantasized how wonderful the reunion would be and never anticipated her daughter would have nothing to do with her. She never even had a chance to explain why and how she happened to be taken from her mother. Samantha was still heart broken to know her baby had died without knowing how much she had been loved.

"I won't let that happen with my granddaughter." Sam talked to herself as she struggled more and more with the now slippery, snow-covered road.

"I'll make up for what I couldn't do for Alexis. I'll tell Father I've found her, and she will come to live with us. I'm going to make a difference in her life." Sam became more and more excited just thinking about the future and continued to talk out loud even though no one was there to hear her.

"I'll just give Father time to adjust to the idea and then I'll bring her home." She knew if she handled things right, it would be just fine because her father did not have the strength to fight his daughter anymore. He spent most of his time in front of the big picture window overlooking the city and had lost most of the orneriness he had as a younger man. Besides, having a young child in the house would liven things up in the Howard Mansion.

Benjamin Howard was an old man now and had mellowed some since his retirement, but he still had his stubborn ways. Sam was slowly taking over the affairs of the family business and knew she would inherit millions when her father passed. She didn't care about the money, but wanted to be sure her granddaughter would be cared for. She would need to contact the family attorney and give him the information he needed to include Sarah in the family trust fund.

As she made her plans for Sarah to come into her life, she was happier than she had ever been. She hummed to herself and smiled knowing it was only a matter of time now until she would have part of Alexis and Alexander with her again.

Her mind was racing with all the plans for the future, and with the distraction, she misjudged her speed going into the curve. The road was now covered with snow and the Mercedes went into a slide. Sam panicked and tried to correct the sliding car that had gone into the oncoming lane. She didn't see the huge snow plow until the last second. Then it was too late to get out of its way. Brakes were useless on the icy road, and the huge vehicle plowed into her car sending it careening over the embankment and down the snow-covered mountain where it landed on its hood. She felt the blood pouring from her head and an awful, searing pain in her legs. Then the pain was gone. All she felt was the chilling cold and then nothing.

Chapter Sixteen

1968

"I would like to propose a toast!" John Peterman said as he held his glass of wine high to set an example for the rest of the guests on the huge redwood deck overlooking the golf course.

"To the most extraordinary, intelligent and beautiful eighteen-year-old in all of Portland. Happy Birthday, Sarah!"

"Happy Birthday!" Everyone chimed in as they touched their wine classes together and sipped to honor Sarah's special day.

"I would like to add to that toast, John." Carol Peterman stood to face Sarah. "To the most wonderful daughter any parent could ever hope for. Thank you for being a part of our lives."

Sarah's eyes filled with tears as she looked around the deck at her friends and realized she was very fortunate. She choked back the tears of gratitude and stood holding the untouched glass of wine that had been poured in her honor.

"Thank you. I don't know how to express my feelings of gratitude and love for you both. You came into my life at a time when I truly thought my life was over. I will be forever grateful to you."

She held her glass high and added, "To John and Carol, my friends, my parents, and my guardian angels."

Sarah put the glass of wine to her lips as the others joined her. This would be her first taste of alcohol. But she couldn't drink. As she breathed in the scent from the wine, the memory of that awful smell came rushing back to her. For a moment she was eight years old again and saw her drunken mother trying to sit upright at the kitchen table the night Hank was killed. Sarah would never forget that night and could never forget that awful smell of alcohol on her mother and father.

She just couldn't drink. She knew it was a celebration of her passing into adulthood, and Petermans' wanted her to feel like an adult, but at this moment, she knew she would never need alcohol to make her feel like an adult. She would never need it for anything and she slowly placed her glass on the table next to her deck chair.

Her behavior went unnoticed by the guests, but Carol watched Sarah and read the expression on her face. Carol knew what she was thinking, and as Sarah glanced her way, she smiled a knowing smile. They had learned to communicate in a very special way over the past ten years. Their relationship was a combination of mother-daughter, sisters and best friends. And now, they just didn't need to speak.

"Everyone grab a plate and get in line. I'm ready to serve my world famous burgers." John jokingly donned an apron and a huge chef's hat and headed for the smoking barbecue grill.

Carol helped him serve the thirty or more guests and soon everyone was taking their seats at the tables set up on the lawn for the birthday celebration. It was a perfect June day with the sun shining and just a tiny breeze sending the faint scent of the blooming azaleas to mingle with the charcoal in the air. Sarah sat on the lawn chair watching the golfers in the distance and let her thoughts drift back in time.

****

It had been nearly ten years ago since the Petermans' came to pick up the pieces of little Sarah's life. She vaguely remembered the day she learned her father was dead, but Carol told her it was normal for a young child to block out devastating things. It had been too much for her young mind to handle.

John and Carol took Sarah into their lives that day and raised her as their own child, comforting and protecting her from the awful situation the cruel twist of fate had caused.

Maybe it was meant to be that Sarah would eventually end up with the Petermans. She loved Carol from the time she met her as her Sunday school teacher and Carol immediately knew that Sarah had found a special place in her heart. So when Sarah became an orphan at the age of eight and one half years old, there was no question in Carol's mind that she and John should become her legal guardians.

It helped that Benton, Idaho was a small town, and the Petermans were well known and very well liked. With no family members in Sarah's life to care for her, it was easy for John and Carol to get the courts to agree to the guardianship of Sarah. No one wanted to see the young girl sent to a foster home. So the paperwork was handled within a week of Harvey Taylor's death, and Sarah legally had a new family.

When John and Carol tried to explain to Sarah that they had become her Legal Guardian, Sarah didn't fully understand and asked if that meant they were her Guardian Angels. And for years, Sarah referred to them in that way.

John made all the arrangements for Harvey's funeral and handled all of the matters of his estate while Carol packed Sarah's things and closed up the old farmhouse. Though Sarah had not remembered many details of that time in her life, she did remember getting into the car with John and Carol that day with Jake clutched in her arms. And she remembered looking out the back window of the car, as they drove down the lane, at the old farmhouse that now had boards covering the windows and doors.

The Petermans did everything they could to make Sarah feel at home. The spare room was completely redecorated and Carol painted the walls in a soft yellow. A new white canopy bed, dresser and nightstand were delivered along with all the bedding in yellow and white with a matching bedside lamp. It was a beautiful and cheerful room that was perfect for a young girl.

Sarah was appreciative and enjoyed the attention but she just couldn't get past the sadness. She pretended to be all right during the day, but at night she often cried herself to sleep as she curled up next to Jake. She missed her father and her old home on the river.

She attended school each day, but her teacher noticed, and told Carol that Sarah was withdrawing into her own little world. Even though she had never been very social, now she rarely spoke to the other children, and she no longer participated in class discussions or projects. She just sat by herself, away from the others, and gazed off into space.

"I don't know what to do for her, John." Carol said to him with concern. "She's so quiet and doesn't want to talk about her feelings. The nightmares seem to be getting worse."

"I know, I heard her again in the night. Do you know what the nightmares are about? Does she tell you anything when you wake her?"

"No, she doesn't talk about them, and she just trembles when I wake her. I don't know what to do except just hold her until she goes back to sleep. It's so sad. She must have so much on her mind. I've not seen her cry since the funeral, and I know that can't be healthy."

"You're right, Honey. If anyone ever had justification to cry a river, it would be Sarah. I can't imagine how devastating it must be to lose both of your parents in such a short time. Maybe she just needs a little time."

"I know you're right, Dear. I just wish I could make it better for her right now. She is such a special little girl."

"You know Carol, maybe Sarah needs more than a pretty room and new clothes to get her mind off the past. Maybe she needs to see someone who can get her to open up and talk about everything that has happened to her."

"That's a good idea, John. Do you have anyone in mind?"

"Not in this part of the country, but I do have an old college buddy in Portland that would be perfect for this situation. Maybe I'll give Jeremy a call."

That phone call caused a chain of events for the Petermans and Sarah. Dr. Jeremy Webster, a child psychiatrist, was immediately interested in Sarah and suggested John and Carol bring her for a visit. At the end of March, during Sarah's spring break from school, the car was packed, and John, Carol, Sarah and Jake drove to Portland,

Oregon. They told Sarah they were going on a vacation to visit some old friends in Portland and then on to see the Oregon coast.

They spent two days in Portland with Jeremy and Sally Webster, so Jeremy would have the chance to observe Sarah and give an opinion of her condition. He spent several hours with Sarah and managed to get her to open up a little.

Jeremy, Sally, John, and Carol sat at the table having dessert, drinking coffee, and looking through the spacious dining room window into the back yard. They watched as Sarah sat on the lawn, petting Jake, and gazing off in the distance.

"See, she just sits there with Jake." Carol said sadly. "Shouldn't an eight-year-old child run and play and be full of energy?"

Sally shook her head, "Well, I'm not the expert, but it doesn't take an expert to know she is one very sad little girl."

"Jeremy, what is your take on this now that you have spent some time with her?" John questioned.

"Well, I certainly believe she has been traumatized by the events of the past year, but there is more to it than that. She shows all the signs of physical and emotional abuse. Did you know much about her parents? Is it possible they were abusive?"

"I don't think so." John replied. "I've never heard any reports of abuse, and people usually talk in a small town."

"Wait a minute." Carol said slowly with a faraway look in her eyes. "I remember Sarah coming to church one time, not long before her mother died, and her face was swollen and bruised. When I questioned her, she acted very strange."

"You may be on to something, Jeremy." John added. "And that could explain the horrible nightmares she has. What do you think we should do?"

"Well, if she was abused by her parents, she is not only struggling to understand their deaths, but why they abused her. She could have all kinds of issues of not being loved and protected, feeling guilty about their deaths, and thinking she may have caused it in some way. I think she needs therapy to deal with it."

"You're probably right. The possibility of abuse does make sense when I think about it." Carol said. "Her mother was a very strange woman. Sometimes she was very friendly, and other times she was cold and almost rude. And come to think of it, I never noticed any affection between Sarah and her mother. And she never talks about her."

"I noticed that too, now that you mention it." John added. "And, I found it strange that so few people attended the funeral service for Alexis. I heard the rumor that she drank too much, but I just thought it was small town gossip.

. "It all adds up, doesn't it?" Sally concluded.

"It sure does. Poor Sarah. She must be living in a very sad and confusing world." Carol looked at John as she shook her head and tears formed at the corners of her eyes. "We've got to help her, John."

"I know, Dear." He replied as he placed his hand on hers. "We will help her. Now that we know what we are dealing with, lets give it some thought."

"I will help you and Sarah any way I can."

"Thank you, Jeremy. We appreciate all you have done."

They left the following day to make good their promise to take Sarah to see the Pacific Ocean. Two hours later they checked into a motel located on the beach in Lincoln City, Oregon.

They took Sarah shopping and found a set of colored pencils and tablets for her. Sarah's eyes lit up when she saw the supplies and immediately put them to use, sketching the ocean and the surrounding scenery. Finally, she had colored pencils for drawing, and she seemed very content to sit with her tablet and draw.

It was a beautiful day, and John and Carol sat on an old piece of driftwood watching Sarah and Jake along the beach while the surf came in and out in the distance. They had already spent three days enjoying the sights and sounds of the ocean and the quaint little town, and enjoyed every minute.

"Don't you hate to leave, John?" Carol said as she watched the waves splash against the shore. "It is so beautiful here."

"Yes, it is. And, it has been good for Sarah. This is the happiest I've seen her."

"Yes, she does seem happy. She has really enjoyed the art supplies, and I think she has a real talent for drawing. It may be a good escape for her."

"I agree." John replied. Maybe we should sign her up for art lessons when we get home.

"John," Carol said thoughtfully. "What would you think of moving to Oregon? Maybe we should get her away from the memories."

And, four months later, they did. John was able to get a transfer with the bank, and Carol graduated from college and accepted a teaching job in Portland. And, best of all, Sarah was able to meet with Dr. Jeremy Webster every week.

Sarah slowly connected with Dr. Jeremy, who was very soft spoken, and gentle, and an expert in child abuse. Within a few weeks, she started to open up and talked to him about how much she loved her Grandmother Sarah. It was the beginning of the healing process for her, and her sessions eventually moved into the relationship with her parents.

The nightmares grew worse for a while, and John and Carol were very concerned that Dr. Jeremy was pushing her too hard. But, he reassured them it was part of the healing process and talking about the nightmares helped Sarah confront her fears. Dr. Jeremy thought they were making good progress.

He focused heavily on he nightmares, and soon she looked forward to telling him what she had dreamed so he could make her understand it. Sarah started talking freely about her father and Grandmother Sarah, but it took many months before she would discuss her mother. It was a big breakthrough once she did, and the nightmares seemed to subside a little.

As Sarah felt more comfortable talking about her mother, Dr. Jeremy asked if she would allow him to include John and Carol in their sessions. Sarah agreed, and it proved to be very beneficial for all of them.

The Petermans learned about the horrible beatings and the verbal abuse from Alexis. They realized Harvey had contributed to the problems by not standing up to his wife and defending his helpless child. They finally understood what this little girl had experienced in her first eight years, and knew it would take a long time to heal the wounds.

The greatest task was to make Sarah realize she was very much wanted and loved, and that she had done nothing to cause her mother's behavior. They were careful not to say anything bad about Sarah's parents, because they knew she would always feel the need to defend them. Instead, they focused on the positive side of making Sarah feel special and whole again. Thank goodness for Grandmother Sarah. She had shown love to Sarah when she was small and that made the healing process easier for her.

The Petermans gave Sarah a wonderful life. They loved her and taught her to love them in return. They spoiled her in many ways but they also taught values and lessons of life that made Sarah grow up to become a kind and caring young woman.

****

Now, at her eighteenth birthday party, the reality of being grown up started to sink in and she felt a surge of excitement. She had been awarded an academic scholarship for college, and she had her whole life ahead of her. Thanks to the love and kindness of John and Carol, she knew she could be anything she wanted to be. She knew she was smart enough, and the old wounds had healed as much as could be expected. She felt very blessed.

John and Carol glanced her way from time to time and they caught one another doing so. They smiled that knowing grin that only a long time married couple could understand. They both knew the thoughts of the other, and that they were very proud of Sarah. She had grown up to be a kind and compassionate person. Not only was she very intelligent and beautiful, she was extremely talented. Their home was full of paintings and drawings that Sarah had done over the years.

Sarah was fair skinned and still had the long white blonde hair she had as a child. Her lovely blue eyes now danced and sparkled and only occasionally showed a trace of the sadness they once had. Her physical beauty was exceptional, and she had an aloofness about her that only caused people to want to get to know her better. She had many friends, but she had shared her childhood secrets with no one except John, Carol and Dr. Jeremy. They hadn't talked about those early days of her life in a long time.

Jeremy and Sally Webster attended her birthday party and had remained close friends with the Petermans. Sarah was grateful for the many years Dr. Jeremy had worked with her and knew she owed so much to him for helping her understand her childhood. She had learned to accept what had happened to her, but still could not forgive her mother.

The guests finished their barbecued hamburgers and Carol cut the birthday cake while Sarah opened her gifts. Most of the gifts were meant to be funny or had something to do with preparing for college, and she had a great time. She noticed John and Carol did not give her a gift while the others were there, but after the last guest departed they explained why.

"Let's all have a seat at the table, shall we?" John took charge and they sat down, each with a cup of tea. "Sarah, years ago we made the decision we would give you this gift on your eighteenth birthday, and that day has finally arrived."

He handed her a large manila envelope with her name on the front. She thought it seemed a little odd for a birthday present, but opened it as John and Carol watched her expression.

"I don't understand. What is this?" She questioned as she looked at the official looking document she held in her hand.

"It is a Warranty Deed, Sarah." John replied. "It is the deed to the house and 20 acres on the Snake River where you lived as a child. It belongs to you now."

"Oh my gosh!" Sarah said with confusion. "The property belongs to me? But, how did you get it? I thought it was sold along time ago."

"Well, it didn't actually sell, but we will explain it all later. There is a lot for you to know."

"And that's not all, Honey." Carol added. "When we closed up the old house, and brought you to live with us, we saved some of your parent's personal things. We knew you would want to have them someday."

"But where are these things now? That was ten years ago, and I've never seen anything from my old home."

"It has been in storage in Benton all these years." John explained. "If you will agree, we would like to take you back to see the old house, and go through the items we stored for you."

"Yes Honey, and on the way, we will explain everything about how we managed to get the property." Carol added.

"Sure, I guess I would like to see it again." Sarah said with outward enthusiasm, even though she felt uneasy about reliving the old memories.

"It's settled then. We will leave in the morning!" Carol said as she got up to clear the table. "It's been a long day. Why don't we call it a night, and get some sleep. Tomorrow we leave for Benton, Idaho."

Chapter Seventeen

It was difficult for Sarah to get to sleep that night. She hadn't thought about the old house in years, and now, she actually owned it. Her mind raced with questions. What would she do with the property? Did she even want it? How would she feel when she saw it again? Could she handle the inevitable memories associated with the old house?

As John and Carol packed the car for the trip to Idaho, Sarah sat in her room watching them from her window. She knew John and Carol meant well, and they must have a reason for wanting her to have the property and wanting her to see some of the possessions again. They had always done what was best for her, and she trusted them completely. They must think this was something she needed to do. And, after all, she was an adult now. She was eighteen.

She tried to reassure herself that she could handle this. It had been a long time ago, and with the help of Dr. Jeremy, and the years of therapy, she thought she had made peace with her early childhood. Still, it never occurred to her that she would revisit her old home, and that visit could cause old memories to resurface. She had never had any desire to see the place. Until now. She felt a slight surge of excitement and then apprehension as she thought about what lay ahead.

When everything was packed and loaded in the car, John, Carol, and Sarah got in and headed east. They drove along the Columbia Gorge and planned to follow the Columbia River until the highway turned southeast toward Idaho, leaving the river behind. Sarah sat silently in the back seat of the spacious Lincoln with the large manila envelope on her lap. After they were well into their journey, and Sarah had been unusually quiet, Carol turned from the front seat to look at her.

"Sarah, we know this trip may be a little difficult for you. We discussed it with Dr. Jeremy and he encouraged us to take you back for a visit."

"Yes, Sweetheart," John said as he glanced in the rear view mirror to catch Sarah's eyes, "He thinks, and we agree with him, that this trip may answer a lot of questions for you and give you some final closure."

"I'm sure you're right, but I'm just a little nervous about seeing it all again. I'm not sure how I will feel after all these years."

"That's certainly understandable but we will be with you, and we will help you through it, Honey," John tried to reassure her.

"Thank you, I know you will." Sarah said as she pulled the Warranty Deed from the envelope and looked at the document for the second time.

"The date on this deed is just yesterday, and it is from you to me. I don't understand. Did you own the property? How did you get it and who did you buy it from?"

"It is a little complicated, Sarah." John explained. "But, we will start from the beginning and tell you all we know."

"We bought your father's property about nine years ago from a man named James Cooper. Mr. Cooper bought it from Ben Jackson." Carol started the story but Sarah interrupted.

"Ben Jackson? How did he get my father's land?" Sarah immediately felt the fear associated with his name from many years ago and memories of his late night visits flashed in her mind.

"Did you know Ben Jackson, Sarah?" John asked.

"Not really, but I knew that my father owed him money, and he killed our dog, Hank." Sarah responded sadly.

"I remember you telling us about your dog, but you never mentioned that someone killed him." Carol said.

"How did he get my father's land?" Sarah asked with just a touch of anger now.

"Well, after your father's accident, I was appointed by the court to handle the estate for your parents." John replied, "When I tried to settle everything, I found a lien against the property. It had been filed by Mr. Jackson the day your father was found drowned in the river."

Carol added, "Apparently, your father signed the papers that authorized him to file the lien. By the time John paid all the bills, the funeral expenses and legal costs for the estate, there was no money to pay Mr. Jackson. We thought about trying to sell the property, but the real estate market was really bad and we knew it would be hard to sell."

"We wanted to keep the property for you to have one day," John explained, "So I went to Mr. Jackson and told him we would personally come up with the money to pay him."

"How much did my father owe him?" Sarah asked.

"It was one thousand dollars plus the interest so he wanted just over twelve hundred dollars to release his lien. I asked him to give us a few months to come up with the money and he agreed. But, when we finally raised the money and called him to handle the paper work, he informed us he had foreclosed on the property and already sold the place to a man named Cooper.

"We were sick about it, Sarah." Carol added. "It didn't seem right that he would go back on his word but it was done and we couldn't do anything about it."

"That doesn't sound fair. How could he just sell our property?"

"It wasn't fair Sarah, but it was legal. Your father had given him the right to foreclose and take the property if he didn't get paid, and that's what he did."

"There wasn't anything for us to do except try to find the new owner and see if he would sell it to us. It took almost one year to find him, convince him to sell and then come up with the money, but we did. We have owned it since that time and waited for your eighteenth birthday, so we could deed it to you."

"It seems like you went to so much trouble. Why was it so important for you to buy the land?" Sarah questioned.

"We thought it should be yours," John answered. "It's a part of your past. It is your legacy, Sarah. Now it's up to you to decide what you should to do with it."

They arrived in Benton ten hours later and found a room at the only motel in the tiny town. It was dark, and they were exhausted from the long trip. They made plans to visit Sarah's old home the following morning.

Sarah woke at five o'clock Oregon time, which was six o'clock Idaho time. She was anxious to see her old home and go to the storage unit where the personal belongings were stored. There was one thing in particular that she wanted to see and hoped she would be able to find it without much trouble. But first, they would visit the property that now belonged to her. It felt strange knowing she actually owned the land, and especially the land that had been in her father's family and passed down to him. It was rightfully hers and she was grateful to the Petermans for making sure she would have it one day.

As the three of them took the road from town and headed for her old home, Sarah felt the emotions set in and knew this might take more courage than she had anticipated. But she was determined to get through it. John and Carol had been right. She needed to have closure.

In the distance, she saw the big bend in the road, near the river, and felt a lump in her throat. This was the place where her father's red truck had gone off the road. This was the place where he drowned ten years ago.

"Please pull off the road." She said as John slowed down to take the big curve.

"Are you sure, Sarah?" Carol asked knowing this was the place Harvey had died.

"Yes, I need to see it."

John pulled into the parking area that was now paved and had picnic tables scattered along the bank of the river. What was once a favorite fishing hole and difficult to drive into was now a lovely picnic area that attracted family gatherings.

Sarah got out of the car and stared at the big, slow moving river. She closed her eyes and imagined what her father must have felt that night as his truck plunged into the cold water. She took a deep breath and tried to hold back the tears, but they escaped at the corners of her eyes and her shoulders shook as she tried not to let anyone see her cry. Carol put her arms around her and held her.

"He was a good man, really he was." Sarah sobbed into Carol's shoulder.

"I'm sure he was, Sweetheart. It's too bad he didn't have more time with you, so he could see what a wonderful daughter he had."

"I loved him." Sarah said as she held onto Carol. "And, I still miss him." She pulled away and walked to the edge of the river, sat down on the ground and stared at the water. After a few minutes, she walked over to the wild flowers growing at the side of the water, pulled several and tossed them into the water.

"Good-bye, Father."

John and Carol waited at the car and watched from a distance as Sarah went through the ritual, and then slowly made her way back to them.

"I'm ready to see the house now." Sarah said as she got into the car and wiped the last of her tears.

A few minutes later, the Lincoln turned off the main road and continued down the dusty old lane that led to the old Taylor house. The undercarriage of the car scraped on the weeds that had taken over from years of no travel. Sarah's first impression was how small the house seemed to her. As a child, she had always thought it was so big, and now she realized it was quite tiny and very much in need of repair.

The windows and doors were covered with boards and John had to pry them from the front door so they could go inside. No one had been inside since the day Petermans took Sarah away. Neither Ben Jackson nor James Cooper ever saw the inside. Jackson had no interest in the house or land, and Cooper's only interest in the property was for the access to the river so he could fish when he came to town.

The inside of the house was dark from lack of sunlight and smelled old and musty. John removed a couple of the boards covering the windows, and Carol opened them to let in the fresh air. Sarah just stood in the living room and let the memories rush through her. She was eight years old again. Her mind's eye saw the fight between her parents and her father beating her mother for losing the money they had saved to pay Jackson. Now she knew it had been one thousand dollars and that was a lot of money for poor people. But was it enough to cause the chain of events that led to the deaths of two people?

She walked into the kitchen, and stopped at the doorway, as more memories came. It was as if time had reversed itself, and it was ten years earlier. She heard her mother yelling at her and saw her mother's face the day she accidentally broke the teacup. She looked at the old woodpile and remembered the sharp whack on her back when her mother beat her with the wood. Tears were forming but she didn't want to give in to them and rushed back out through the front door toward the old barn. She had to get some fresh air and get these bad memories out of her head.

The dilapidated old barn hadn't changed much over the years, but it was covered with dust, and the cobwebs were thick. Sarah stood at the door, not wanting to go near the cobwebs. She still had a fear of spiders that she associated with those horrible times she was forced to stay in the locked cellar. She looked around the barn, and for a moment heard the sounds of the farm animals, and saw her father showing her how to milk the cow. She smiled to herself, and wondered if she would ever milk another cow. There hadn't been much use for that knowledge growing up in a suburb of Portland.

Then she turned to face the old potato cellar. She had put this off until the last, afraid of the memories it would bring. She stared at it for several minutes, and gave a start when Carol and John walked up behind her and touched her shoulder.

"Let's go in, Sarah." Carol told her as John opened the door and held it for them.

"I'm not sure I can." Sarah said softly. "I hated it in there."

"I know, Sweetheart. But John and I will be with you. It is something you need to do. You need to put it behind you."

Carol held her hand as they entered the dark cellar. John was already at the bottom of the stairs and had cleared the cobwebs for them. He held a powerful flashlight and illuminated the stairs as Sarah slowly edged into the damp cellar. As John moved the flashlight around the tiny room, Sarah saw the pile of potato sacks and the old orange crate. The old feelings of terror came back and she felt slightly queasy as she looked around the tiny, dark room. She put her arms around herself as if she could comfort the little eight-year-old girl that still lived deep inside.

Neither John nor Carol spoke, but just watched Sarah as their eyes slowly adjusted to the dim light. Sarah stood for several minutes before she took a deep breath and started to speak.

"I slept here on the sacks when my mother locked me in. I thought if I fell asleep, I wouldn't feel the spiders crawl on me." Sarah spoke softly and slowly, without looking at them, and John and Carol knew she was no longer speaking to them.

"I was just a little girl. How could you put me in a place like this? How could you beat me as though I were an animal?" She said louder now as she looked upward to the familiar crack in the ceiling.

"How could anyone be so cruel?" She sat on the orange crate, put her face in her hands and sobbed. "You were my mother! You were supposed to love me and protect me! How could you do it?"

John and Carol listened as Sarah talked to her dead mother, and they both felt their own tears fall as they witnessed and felt the pain Sarah felt from that awful time in her life. They wanted to get her out of this place, but they knew she needed to be here one more time. Sarah continued to sob as Carol stroked her long hair to comfort her.

"It's okay, Sarah. It's okay to be mad. What she did was wrong. You didn't deserve it. It was never your fault, Honey. She was a sick woman, and she needed help. But, you have to try to forgive her and move on."

"I can't forgive her. And I can't forget what she did to me." Sarah replied as she stood and wiped her eyes. She was emotionally exhausted from the memories and the tears.

"I know that all the years of therapy should make it better, but now that I'm here, and I see this awful place, I just can't understand how she could do it."

Even though John and Carol had heard many of the stories of the child abuse during the family sessions with Sarah and Dr. Jeremy, they could not entirely visualize what Sarah had been through, until now. Seeing the dark cellar and knowing that this precious young woman had been beaten and locked in here was very disturbing. The three stood with their arms around one another, and their own thoughts in that awful place that held the secrets of the Taylor family.

I'm ready to go." Sarah said as she pulled away from them. "Please, I want to go now."

As they walked away from the cellar, Sarah stopped and turned back to take one more look. She had done it. She had faced the potato cellar, the monster that had given her nightmares for many years. She felt better for a moment, and then she felt a rush of anger. She picked up an old tire iron that was leaning up against the barn and walked back to the cellar. John and Carol watched as Sarah used the tire iron to hit the latch on the cellar door. She smashed into it over and over until the latch flew to pieces and onto the ground.

Chapter Eighteen

John opened the door to the storage shed and turned on the dusty overhead light. The wattage was low, and the sunlight was bright outside, so it took a few seconds for their eyes to adjust. Everything was covered with sheets and blankets to keep the dust off, and Carol quickly removed the coverings so Sarah could see the meager possessions they had stored for her.

There was the chrome kitchen table and three matching chairs, a green sofa and chair, a full size bed and a twin bed, two dressers, a chest of drawers, and several boxes. More memories flooded into Sarah's mind as she moved through the storage shed, touching and looking at the items. Everything was so old and worn.

"It's strange, isn't it," Sarah said thoughtfully, "What you remember as a child? I always thought we had nice things in our home, but this is all so old and ugly."

"It's been ten years, Sarah. Everything is older now. These things were not so bad ten years ago." Carol tried to reassure her even as she thought to herself that Sarah was right.

Sarah couldn't help but feel disappointed. This was all that was left of her parents. But, still she kept looking around. She had not seen the one item she had thought about for years, and she really needed to find it. She opened boxes of old clothes, linens, dishes and tools, but it wasn't there. When she thought she had gone through everything, she looked behind a stack of boxes and saw the outline of a chair.

"May I borrow the flashlight, please? I can't see what's in the corner back here."

"Sure, I'll get it, Sweetheart." John said as he hurried to the car.

SUSAN KAY

"Can I help you find something, Sarah?" Carol asked. She had watched Sarah rummage through box after box and not show much interest in what she found, other than the box of photo albums.

"My mother had a music box......" She started to explain as John turned the flashlight on and lit up the back corner of the storage area.

"And there it is!" Sarah saw it just as she spoke, and quickly moved the boxes away so she could get to it. It was sitting on the old rocking chair, nearly hidden beneath the afghan made by Grandmother Sarah. She stopped short for a moment as she recalled the many times Grandmother rocked her in that old rocking chair and covered her with the afghan as she fell asleep on her lap.

"What do you want to do with all this, Sarah?" Carol asked.

"I would like to take a couple of things with me." Sarah said as she turned to John and Carol. "I don't want anything other than the rocking chair, the afghan, that box of photo albums, and this music box. We can give everything else to the Salvation Army or who ever wants it."

Sarah picked up the music box and ran her fingers over the carved angels on the top to wipe off the dust. "She never let me near this. The one time I touched it, she got mad at me, and told me never to touch it again. I always wanted to hold it and listen to the pretty music."

Sarah walked out of the dark storage area and sat the music box on the top of the car. "It's locked. I wonder if I can find a key for it."

"Turn it upside down and look on the bottom, Sarah." Carol said anxiously. "I remember finding the key when we cleared out the house and I taped it to the bottom. I hope it's still there."

"Here is it!" Sarah exclaimed. "Oh, I can't believe it. You don't know how many times I've thought about this box. My father gave it to my mother as a wedding gift and she kept her personal things inside. Do you think they might still be there?"

"I don't know why not. We packed everything just the way we found them. I remember opening the box and seeing a stack of letters. Why don't we go back to the motel, and you can take your time

134

going through them?"

"That sounds like a good idea. I didn't know much about my mother. Do you think this box might have some answers for me?"

"I hope so, Sarah." Carol replied. "Come on now. Let's get John to lock up everything. I'm anxious for you to see what's in your mother's music box."

Back at the motel, Sarah placed the music box on the small table in the corner of the room. She used a washcloth to wipe off the dust and carefully inserted the corner of the cloth into the tiny crevasses of the carved wood. Once it was clean, she pulled the hardened tape from the key on the bottom and put it into the tiny keyhole. She wound the turnkey at side of the box and took a deep breath as she opened the angel-covered lid. The music started to play.

"I can't believe it still works."

"It is playing Edelweiss, isn't it?" Carol asked.

"Yes. I always thought it was so pretty when I was little. I used to sit outside Mother's bedroom door so I could listen to it and hope she wouldn't catch me there."

She listened to the music and stared at the stack of letters she had taken from the inside of the box. Now that it was empty, she could see the beautiful purple velvet lining and the mirror on the inside of the lid. She turned her attention back to the stacks of letters.

"I don't know where to begin. There are so many of them. Do you want to help me sort? This may take a while."

"Sarah, if you don't mind, John and I need to take care of some business downtown. So why don't you stay here and take time going through the letters. We will be back in a couple of hours."

"Sure, I'll be fine." Sarah replied in a daze. Her mind was on those letters, and she was anxious to get started.

Once they were in the car, John said, "We don't have any business, Carol. Why did you want us to leave? Shouldn't we be there for her right now?"

"No, John, she needs to do this alone. I don't know what she will find in those letters, but she needs to read them by herself. Don't worry, she will be fine."

"You're a good mother, Carol. You always know what's best for her. I wish we could have had a dozen kids."

"So did I, John, but we were blessed to have Sarah and I'll settle for grandchildren someday. Now let's go find a diner, so you can buy me a piece of pie and a cup of coffee."

Chapter Nineteen

Sarah began her task by sorting through the stack of letters and noticed most of them had the same handwriting, which she put into one pile. As she opened the first one and started to read it, she realized it was one of several love letters to her mother, written by her father, Harvey, and the dates showed a period of about six months, just before their marriage in 1950.

As she read, she learned about their courtship and the early part of their relationship. It was obvious her father had been very much in love with her mother. After reading several letters, Sarah realized her mother had been seeing another man. Many of the letters referred to the "Jerk" and how he could never make Alexis as happy as Harvey could. Sarah wondered whom her father was referring to, but a name was never mentioned.

She was touched by the tenderness her father had demonstrated in the letters and was especially interested in the last letter he had written in February of 1950.

My Dear Alexis,

I can't get you out of my mind. I love you and want to marry you as soon as possible. I have told Mother that you are pregnant, and the baby is mine. She has given her blessing. You will never convince me that the baby does not belong to me and even if it does belong to the "Jerk", I will love it because it is a part of you. I only hope that the baby will have your eyes and your smile for I couldn't help but love it. Please say you will be my wife and say goodbye to him. I promise to make you happy.

Harv

Sarah starred at the letter as her thoughts raced. She recalled the night her mother died when she screamed at Harvey that Sarah wasn't his baby. Her father had gone insane when he heard it, but Alexis had said she didn't mean it. Now Sarah wondered if she did mean it. What if Harvey wasn't her real father? She had loved him and he had loved her. What if it had all been a lie? She knew her mother was capable of lying. She had been capable of many awful things. After all, she had been seeing two men at the same time and wasn't sure which one had made her pregnant.

Sarah felt sick at her stomach. If Harvey wasn't her father, then who was? Who was the "Jerk" Harvey referred to in the letters? And if Harvey wasn't her father, that meant Grandmother Sarah wasn't her real grandmother.

Surely God could not be that cruel. He couldn't take away the small amount of security she had as a child in knowing she had a grandmother and father that loved her. It was awful to think the only person she was really related to was one who beat her and never wanted her. Even with all the therapy Sarah had been through to build her self-esteem, and all the love she had been given by John and Carol, she felt so alone now.

Maybe reading these letters hadn't been such a good idea. She had been so certain that she would find some answers in the music box and now she felt such disappointment. She put her head down on the table and started to cry. But the tears didn't last long. They were replaced with anger. She got up, washed her face and decided to finish going through the stack. Maybe the answers were there after all. She had to keep looking.

As she sorted through the next stack of letters and papers, one caught her eye. It was crinkled and appeared to have been crushed and than straightened and folded to be placed in the box. As she unfolded the paper, she knew immediately what is was. It was the suicide letter from her mother. It was the letter her father held in his hand the morning he told Sarah her mother was dead. Sarah took a deep breath as she the read the short letter in her mother's familiar handwriting.

> *Harv,*
>
> *I was so happy when you asked me to marry you, because I knew someone finally loved me. I'm sorry I never learned to love you in return. You deserved to be loved. I have made such a mess of my life. You and Sarah will be better off without me.*
>
> *Alexis*

Sarah placed the letter on the table and sighed. She felt sorry for this woman. Carol was right. She had been a sick woman, and she couldn't love. It wasn't just Sarah. She couldn't love anyone, not even the man she married. Sarah didn't feel like crying this time. It was as though she had just been told a story about a stranger. She felt sorry for her, but she couldn't relate to her. She couldn't imagine not being able to love the people in your life. When Sarah thought of how much she loved John and Carol and her friends, she couldn't believe this woman, who was unable to love, had been her mother.

She continued through the stack of papers and found a letter, postmarked in Seattle, Washington, about one month before Alexis had died. The envelope was made of heavy, colored paper that looked very expensive. Sarah opened it to find matching colored stationary in lovely handwriting.

> *Dear Alexis,*
>
> *This letter may come as a shock to you after all this time and I can assure you it is something that I have wanted to be able to write for many, many years.*
>
> *I can't imagine how you must feel as you read this and I wish with all my heart I could tell you this in person, but I want you to have some time to absorb what I am about to tell you.*
>
> *I am your mother. I gave birth to you in Seattle on November 3, 1929 and gave you the name of Alexis.*

> *My name is Samantha Howard and I live in Seattle*
> *where I have an art gallery called The Alexis Gallery,*
> *named for you.*
>   *I have enclosed my address and phone number. More*
> *than anything in the world, I would like to meet you*
> *and your family. I have so much to tell you and we have*
> *so many lost years to try and recover. Please call me.*
>   *Samantha Howard*

Sarah's mouth dropped open as she read the letter for a second and third time. It was amazing! If this was true, Sarah had a grandmother in Seattle. Why hadn't her mother ever mentioned this letter? It had been written a month before she killed herself. Did she ever respond to this woman? Was it really her mother? It had to be. She knew her name and her birth date. She had even named her art gallery after Alexis. And why hadn't this woman contacted Sarah. This was ten years later.

Sarah tried to control the emotional roller coaster she felt in her stomach. In just a short time she had gone from not knowing if her Grandmother Sarah was her real grandmother to the possibility that she had a grandmother in Seattle. She took a deep breath and got up to get a drink of water. She wished John and Carol would come back. She needed to talk to someone about all she had learned.

She shuffled through several other letters from old friends and boyfriends of Alexis without any more startling revelations. Being tired from reading the stacks of letters, and seeing name after name of unknown senders, she didn't bother to check the return address on the final letter. Until, after she read it.

Alexis,
>   *I know you have been seeing Harvey Taylor and I*
> *know you are pregnant. You should have told me. I am*
> *willing to try to work things out with you. If the baby*
> *is mine, I will marry you and do the right thing.*
>   *BJ*

"BJ. Who the heck was BJ?" Sarah was now talking to herself as she picked up the envelope and turned it over, searching for the return address. The faded return address read:
Ben Jackson
Benton, Idaho.

Chapter Twenty

John and Carol sat in the tiny motel room giving their full attention to Sarah as she told them about the contents of the letters.

"I have such mixed emotions!" Sarah explained as she paced back and forth holding the four letters that had shaken her world.

"Ben Jackson could be my real father, and this Samantha Howard could be my grandmother. I'm excited that there might be a grandmother out there I never knew, but sad to think that maybe Grandmother Sarah wasn't my real grandmother." Sarah rambled now as her eyes filled with tears. "I can't stand the possibility of that awful man being my father. I've never said this to anyone, but I think he killed my father. I think he ran him off the road that night."

"Sarah, you never mentioned that before. What makes you think he was responsible for Harvey's death?" John asked.

"Just before he left the house that night, my father got a phone call. He acted very strange and left in a hurry, saying he had to go see a friend. He knew I didn't want to be left alone at night, and if he really did need to see a friend, he would have taken me with him. I think that phone call was from Ben Jackson. He wanted his money."

"Honey, the sheriff told me there was no reason to suspect fowl play. He said the road was icy, and the truck was probably going too fast when it went around the corner at the Big Bend."

"I have to know!" Sarah said with agitation. "I have to know if he had something to do with the accident, and I have to know if he is my father."

"Sarah, sometimes we are better off not knowing these things." Carol tried to calm her down. "Harvey was your father. He loved you and raised you for eight years. That's what makes a father."

"I will never be able to go through my life not knowing for sure.

Don't you see? I have to know!"

"Then we will take you to see Ben Jackson." John said as he glanced at Carol. "I agree with Sarah. She has to know the truth."

"But don't you see, you may never know the truth. All you have are some old letters. This Ben Jackson may not even be around anymore. He may not even be alive."

Carol was trying to protect Sarah from a painful situation and was concerned for her emotional well being. It was a lot for an eighteen-year-old girl to handle in one day. It was a lot for anyone to handle in one day.

"Well, it won't take long to find out if Jackson is still around here. Let's try the phone book." John opened the book and found his name. "Still here, and he still has an office on 2nd Avenue, just where I met with him about the property ten years ago. Let's go talk to him, Sarah."

Chapter Twenty One

The Lincoln, carrying John, Carol, and Sarah, pulled into the parking lot and parked in front of the small office building. The sign on the door read *Jackson Enterprises*, and a receptionist sat at a desk in the big front window.

"Are you sure you want to do this, Sarah?" Carol asked.

"Yes." Sarah replied as she stared at the office.

"I'll go with you." John said as he opened the door and started to get out.

"No!" Sarah said. "I want to do this by myself. Please wait here for me. I'll be fine."

John slowly sat back down in the car and closed the door. "Okay, Honey. We'll be here if you need us."

Sarah put her shoulders back, walked into the office and asked to see Mr. Jackson. The receptionist didn't ask her name and simply told her to have a seat as she got up from her chair and walked down the hallway.

The office was clean, yet sparsely decorated with outdated furniture. The coffee table was covered with magazines that were worn and torn. The walls were covered with scenic pictures of the Idaho mountains and a walnut and glass cabinet was full of bowling trophies.

Sarah was nervous and forced herself to take a deep breath to relax. She would finally see Ben Jackson. She would meet the man who had given her nightmares, killed her father and her dog, Hank. She would see the man who could be her real father.

"You can go in now." The receptionist said as she came back to the seating area. "His office is at the end of the hall."

"Thank you." Sarah replied as she stood. She hoped she looked more confident than she felt. She trembled as she turned to walk down the hall. The door at the end of the hall seemed miles away. She hesitated, with second thoughts about asking John and Carol to wait in the car. Maybe she should ask them to come inside with her. John was so good in situations like this. He had such a level head. But, Sarah scolded herself, and reminded herself once again, that she was an adult. She could do this. She had to do this! She had so many questions for this man. She just hoped he had the answers.

"I'm Ben Jackson." The man said as he rose from his big leather chair. He extended his hand and Sarah backed away. She didn't want to shake his hand. This was the awful man she had hated since she was eight years old.

"What can I do for you, young lady?"

Sarah was immediately thrown. This was not what she expected. He was a well-dressed, handsome man with gray hair, and looked to be about forty-five years old. He wasn't nearly as big as she remembered seeing in the dark driveway that night at her home. And, he seemed nice.

"Miss? Are you okay?" He asked, and Sarah realized she had not spoken, and had only been staring.

"Oh, ah, yes. I'm fine."

"What can I do for you?" He repeated.

Sarah composed herself and took a deep breath. "My name is Sarah Taylor. My parents were Harvey and Alexis Taylor. They both died about ten years ago."

"Well, I'll be darned! Little Sarah Taylor! You are all grown up. I can't believe it! Won't you please have a seat, Sarah?" He motioned to the chair as he returned to his. "I knew your parents and I am sorry for your loss. You know, I saw your father the night his truck went into the river, and he was killed. Of course I didn't know he had died until a couple of days later. I had just recorded a lien on your house, and stopped for a beer when I heard the news. I felt really bad about it, and even drove out to the river to see where it happened. I watched them drag his old pickup out of the river that day."

Again, Sarah was thrown. This man was admitting right up front that he saw her father the day he died. "Where did you see my father that night?"

"We met at the Blue Moon Bar and took care of some business for about thirty minutes, and then he left. Said he was in a hurry to get home and he didn't even have a beer."

"My father owed you money."

"Yes, he did. But he couldn't pay me and I had given him a couple of extensions. I knew he wouldn't have the money to pay me that night, so I prepared a note for him to sign that mortgaged his property. He was going to start making payments to me, just like he would at a bank, but he never got the chance. Since I didn't get my money, I had to foreclose and take the property."

Jackson almost seemed embarrassed as he continued, "I'm in the business of loaning money and I had to be paid. The loan was long over due."

Sarah felt herself soften a little and then silently reminded herself that she was here to confront this enemy, not befriend him. "How do I know you didn't run him off the road that night?" Sarah asked defensively. "How do I know you didn't kill him because he didn't pay you on time? I know you killed our dog! I was there the night you came to our house and threatened us."

Sarah realized she was talking too fast and she was angry with herself for showing too much emotion. She didn't want him to see any weakness in her. She was here to challenge him and meant to be strong. Ben Jackson was taken aback by her assertiveness, but understood this young woman needed some answers. He felt sorry for her.

He made his voice soften and spoke slowly while he looked directly into her eyes. "Sarah, I'm sorry about all that. I'm not proud of my behavior in those days. I drank too much, and I had a loud mouth."

He continued to talk softly and slowly to calm Sarah. "And, I didn't mean to kill your dog. I really felt awful about that. He attacked me when I got out of the car that night, and I kicked him to get him off me. I must have kicked him in just the right spot because he didn't move again. I never meant to kill him."

"And, Sarah," He continued, "I never left the bar the night I met with your father until my wife came to pick me up. I didn't even have a car that night. My wife dropped me off while she went to a bridge party and picked me up on her way home. I didn't run Harvey off the road, Sarah, and I didn't kill him. He just had an unfortunate accident."

"Then why did you come to our house and threaten us?"

"In those days, when I got drunk, I had a terrible temper and did stupid things. I was just blowing smoke that night and trying to be tough. I just wanted to scare him and maybe I was a little jealous that Alexis had chosen him instead of me. Harvey was a good man. He meant to pay me, but he was down on his luck and your mother's gambling didn't help their situation."

"How did you know about my mother's gambling?" Sarah was again surprised by the information he offered so freely.

"I knew your mother along time ago." He said as he looked off to see the memories in his mind. "We dated until she met your father, and then she broke up with me. She claimed I drank too much, and she was right. But while I drank, she gambled and I think it finally got the best of her. I loaned her money all the time, even after she married Harvey. But, she never paid me back, and I finally had to refuse to give her any more. She stopped gambling right after you were born, but a few years later she started again and got into a little trouble."

"You mean, you gave her money, knowing she was gambling it away?"

"Yes, but not for long. Once I got married, my wife put her foot down, so I didn't give Alexis any more money. Your mother did okay for awhile, but about a year before she died, she started gambling heavily again, and your father came to me and asked for a loan to cover the losses."

"Why would you loan money to my father?"

"Because, I loved your mother, and I felt sorry for her. It was my way of staying in her life. And once I got to know Harvey, I started to feel sorry for him too, even if he stole my girl and called me a Jerk." Ben chuckled now at the memory.

"You knew he called you a Jerk?"

"Yeah, I thought it was funny until Alexis told me she was going to marry him. Then it wasn't so funny anymore."

Sarah wanted to ask more questions about her mother and father, but again reminded herself why she was here and charged ahead with the main reason for her visit.

"My mother was pregnant when she married my father. You knew she was pregnant. I saw the letter you wrote to her telling her you would marry her."

"Yes, I did. I really did love her, but I was so messed up with the drinking that I didn't plead my case very well."

Sarah looked directly into his eyes and asked, "Mr. Jackson, are you my real father?"

He looked at her for a moment, and then stood to look out the window behind his desk. Sarah took a deep breath and closed her eyes.

"When your mother told me she was pregnant, I was upset, because I didn't want to get married right then. We had broken up by that time and she had been seeing Harvey off and on for a while, and I was mad about it. Harvey chased her and wouldn't let her alone. I think he really loved her, and when he found out she was pregnant, he insisted they get married. I think it was the easy way for Alexis, and I don't think she ever knew for sure if her baby belonged to me or to Harvey."

Sarah was on the edge of her seat and felt her shoulders drop in despair. "So, you really don't know if I am your daughter?"

"Now that I have met you, I wish you could be." He sat on the edge of his desk and looked at Sarah with kind eyes.

"I'm a changed man now, Sarah. I have a good business, make a decent living, and I haven't had a drink in many years. Once your mother died, I realized she had such a hold over me that I couldn't really live my life. I married a wonderful woman. It just took me a few years to appreciate her."

Sarah wondered why he was telling her all these things, and why he didn't just give her a straight answer. She needed to know if he was her father. And, she decided, he wasn't such a bad man after all. Maybe he just didn't know the answer.

"My wife helped me stop drinking, and we decided to start a family of our own. We tried for five years before we finally gave up and went to see a specialist. Turns out, I had a childhood illness that left me sterile. I couldn't make my wife pregnant. There is no way I can be your father, Sarah. Your real father was Harvey Taylor."

Sarah's head dropped to her chest as she breathed in a sigh of relief. He had answered her questions.

Chapter Twenty Two

John donated the items in storage to the local Salvation Army and arranged to have the rocking chair sent to their home in Portland. The afghan, box of photos, and music box sat in the back seat with Sarah as they started their trip back to Portland.

Sarah tried to absorb all she had learned in the two short days they spent in Benton. Harvey was her father, and Grandmother Sarah was her grandmother. She knew that for sure now, and she was so pleased. And, she was glad she had finally met Ben Jackson. She had faced her childhood nightmares, and it felt good. Her mind was free and happy. She owned the twenty acres in Benton and had decided to keep it. She had a plan in her mind about what she would do with it, but knew it would take a lot of planning and a lot of money. She would have to be patient. In the meantime, she had one more letter to follow up on. She wanted to meet Samantha Howard.

"How far is it to Seattle from Portland?" Sarah asked as they crossed the Idaho border and headed into Oregon.

"Not far, probably about one hundred and seventy five miles." John replied. "Why do you ask?"

"I want to meet my grandmother. I have to know why she gave my mother away and why she never contacted me after Mother died."

"I agree, Sarah. It seems so strange that she went to the trouble of finding your mother and never bothered to come see her. It just doesn't add up. Why don't you try to write to her when we get home?"

"I have a better idea." John added. "Let's drive there now. It can't be more than four hundred miles from here. We can head northwest, by way of Yakima, and be in Seattle by tonight. I have some vacation days coming, so I don't have to be back to work right away. I think its time Sarah gets the answers to all of her questions."

Sarah was the first one to wake the next morning. They were in a high-rise hotel in downtown Seattle. In the daylight they could see the Space Needle in the distance and the green rolling hills of the city. It was a beautiful day and Sarah couldn't wait to get started. She pulled the envelope from her bag and reread the letter written by Samantha Howard. The telephone number was there. All Sarah had to do was pick up the phone and dial the number.

But, she wouldn't do that. She wanted to see this woman in person. She had to see her and couldn't risk refusal over the phone. Then, a thought came to her. What if she had moved? After all, it had been ten years since the letter had been written. Sarah quickly dressed. She would just take the chance. She would go to the address on the envelope.

John and Carol insisted they go with her. They refused to let her go to a strange house by herself and even though she wanted to do this alone, she agreed they were right. Rather than try to locate the address in the big city, they hailed a cab and instructed the driver to take them there.

"Oh, you mean the Howard Mansion? Beautiful place! Do you know Mr. Howard?" The cab driver tried to be friendly.

"No, not really." John replied with hesitation and not wanting to share their business with the stranger. "Do you know him, this Mr. Howard?" John assumed this must be the husband of Samantha Howard.

"Oh, I've never met him, but just heard about him for years. Big in the timber business in his day. You in the timber business?"

"No, I am in banking." John replied and changed the subject. "Do we have far to go?"

"Just a mile or so. It sits at the top of that hill overlooking Puget Sound." The cab driver pointed ahead and to his left. "You'll have quite the view of the city from up there."

The guard at the entrance called the mansion to announce their arrival. As they drove into the big circle drive, all three gasped as they saw the huge mansion.

"Here we are. Shall I wait for you?"

"Yes, please do. We are not sure how long it will take." John said as he opened the door.

"Please, let me go." Sarah said. "This may not even be the right place."

"Oh sure it is." The cab driver interrupted. "This is the Howard Mansion, and Mr. Howard still lives here. I didn't know anything about the missus, but heard Mr. Howard was a mean SOB. But I guess you have to be mean to protect all that money."

"Just give me a minute. I'll be right back." Sarah directed to John and Carol. She knew the driver was just being helpful, but she wished they had brought their own car now. He was making her nervous.

Sarah got out of the car and walked toward the massive front door of the mansion. She stopped, looked back at the taxi, and took in the view of the city and water below. It was breath taking. She smiled at John and Carol to let them know she was all right and turned to ring the doorbell.

An older woman, dressed in a nurse's uniform, came to the door and opened it just enough to see Sarah. Visitors were rare at the mansion, and she was surprised to see this pretty young girl standing there. She just stared at Sarah without speaking.

"Good morning." Sarah started. "My name is Sarah Taylor and I would like to see Samantha Howard, please."

The nurse had worked for Mr. Howard for many years and was taken back at the request of the young woman. She didn't know how to respond and just said, "Ah, please, just wait here."

Sarah thought her behavior was strange and felt uneasy at how the woman had looked at her, as though she was almost frightened.

Several minutes went by, and Sarah stood waiting at the entrance while John and Carol watched from the car.

"Mr. Howard will see you." The nurse announced when she returned. "Are you alone?" She asked as she looked at the taxicab suspiciously.

"No, my parents are in the car." Sarah replied.

"Please have them come in. Tell them to dismiss the taxi. We will call for another one when the time comes."

Sarah quickly told John and Carol to join her, and they were led into a massive entry hall. They were stunned at the beauty and elegance of the house. Even though it was old, it was immaculate, and Sarah thought it looked like something out of a magazine. It was obvious the owner was very wealthy.

The nurse directed them into a huge study with picture-frame paneling and two full walls of leather bound books. A massive fireplace filled the wall next to the hand carved desk and full-length windows offered a lovely view of the surrounding gardens.

The nurse continued to stare at Sarah, but she did not speak. She finally invited them to sit in the deep leather chairs that faced the desk, and she left the room. She returned pushing an old man in a wheel chair. She guided him behind the desk, watching Sarah the whole time, and then excused herself.

"My name is Benjamin Howard." He squinted as he looked at them and it was obvious he could not see clearly. "I understand you have asked to see my daughter, Samantha. May I ask, what is your business with her?"

Sarah was immediately intimidated by the gruff old man and couldn't respond. It slowly sank in that this man was not the husband of Samantha Howard, but the father, and that meant he could be her great-grandfather.

John took charge and replied. "My name is John Peterman and this is my wife Carol and our daughter Sarah. We have a letter from Samantha Howard and we would like to speak with her directly, if you don't mind."

"May I see the letter?"

"I think it would be best if we spoke with her about it, Sir." John was trying to be respectful and not sure the contents of the letter should be shared with this man. "Is your daughter here?"

"No, Mr. Peterman, my daughter is not here." He spoke in a softer tone now and hesitated before he continued. "Samantha is dead. She died about ten years ago."

"I'm very sorry Mr. Howard, we didn't know."

"What did you want with Samantha?" He asked. "What's this

about a letter."

Sarah gathered her courage now and stood to speak as she pulled the letter from her purse. "Mr. Howard, we think your daughter was my grandmother. Here, please read the letter."

Benjamin put on his glasses and reached across the desk to take the letter from Sarah. He looked directly into her face as she leaned toward him and placed the letter in his hand.

"Oh, my God." The letter shook in his hand as he stared at Sarah. "You have her eyes and her beautiful hair." His voice trembled as he softly spoke. "You look just like her. You look just like my Samantha."

He continued to stare as Sarah looked closely at him. It was so strange. This man had facial features similar to her mother, Alexis. There was no doubt that he was her great-grandfather.

He read the letter and than read it again as his eyes filled with tears. "She never forgot, did she? She never let her go."

"What do you mean, Mr. Howard?" John asked.

It took a moment for him to respond, and he had a far away look in his eyes. "Sometimes we do things that we think are right at the time and don't stop to think of the consequences of those actions. I made a terrible mistake." He said as his voice cracked and his body shook from trying to hold back tears.

"We all make mistakes, Mr. Howard." Carol said. He was visibly upset, and she was worried about him. "Perhaps we should talk about this some other time. I know Sarah has a lot of questions, and I'm sure you do as well. But we can come back later, can't we, John?"

Sarah wanted to ask him more questions, but she agreed with Carol and felt sorry for this old man. Benjamin Howard was obviously very upset. "Maybe I should get the nurse."

"Yes, Sarah. That's a good idea." John replied, now very worried about him as well. He looked pale and was starring at Sarah with tears in his eyes.

"Please don't leave." Benjamin begged. "Just give me a few minutes and I'll be fine. "Please just ask her to get my pills."

Sarah ran for the nurse who obviously had been listening just outside the door. She quickly brought in the medicine to calm him down and assured the guests he would be fine. "He doesn't have many visitors anymore. He certainly never expected any of this."

She explained to let them know she had heard the conversation. "I know. It certainly surprised me. Sarah, when I first saw you, I thought I had seen a ghost. It was like looking at Samantha again."

"We certainly didn't mean to cause any trouble." Carol said.

"Oh, it's no trouble." The nurse replied. "By the way, I didn't introduce myself. My name is Nancy Carson. This is the most excitement we've had in a long time." She was fussing around him with obvious concern.

"Maybe we should go." John stood as Carol nodded and stood with him.

"Nonsense," Nancy replied. "He will be just fine. "Mr. Howard, why don't we have your guests join you for lunch. I'll show them around the grounds while you rest for a while, and then you can talk some more. How does that sound?"

"That would be nice." He answered with labored breathing and the nurse wheeled him out of the room.

"Please wait here, I will be back in a few minutes."

"Wow!" Sarah exclaimed. "I can't believe this. It is so amazing. He is really my great-grandfather."

"I have a feeling we are going to learn a lot before this day is over." John added.

Nancy came back to get them and told them Mr. Howard was resting in his room. She took them on a tour of the mansion, and the gardens surrounding it. It was magnificent. She explained how she had worked for Mr. and Mrs. Howard for fifteen years and had not only cared for Mr. Howard, but also Mrs. Howard. She told them she had known Samantha, who was a kind and wonderful woman, just like her mother, Ellen Howard.

When they stopped in the formal living room, Nancy pointed to a portrait. "This was Samantha Howard when she was twenty years old. The portrait was painted in Paris by one of her friends. You can see why Mr. Howard was so shocked when he saw you, Sarah. You look just like her."

"Oh my gosh!" Sarah cried as she looked at the painting. "It was her! She was the lady at the funeral! I remember she came toward Father and me and held out her hand. I remember those eyes, and I remember watching her get into her car."

"Unbelievable." John said, shaking his head.

"She knew about me. She came to the funeral and saw me. I wonder why she didn't let us know she was there."

"We will never know, Sarah. The answer to that questioned died with her."

"Nancy, how did Ms. Howard die?" Carol asked.

"It was a car accident. Her car went out of control on an icy road and was hit by a snowplow. She was on her way back from a trip to Idaho. I believe it was in January or February of 1959."

"That was about the time of your father's funeral, Sarah. She must have been at the funeral and was killed on her way back home."

"How sad for her." Carol remarked. "She never got to meet her daughter or granddaughter."

Sarah couldn't take her eyes off the painting. "She was so pretty, wasn't she?"

"Yes, she was." Nancy replied. "Her death nearly destroyed Mr. Howard. She was such a great lady and very talented! She was an artist, you know. I will show you some of her work later on."

At the end of the tour, she took them into a separate wing of the mansion. As she unlocked the doors, she explained where she was taking them. It was the living quarters for Samantha.

"She had an art gallery in downtown Seattle called *The Alexis Gallery.*" Nancy explained. "After her death, they closed it and brought all of her personal paintings here."

John, Carol, and Sarah walked into the apartment. The walls were covered with paintings of toddlers, little girls, teenagers, and finally young women.

"We never understood why she painted all of these and refused to sell them. There are more than twenty paintings and they were all done in November of every year." Nancy explained. Notice the dates at the bottom of each painting and how all of the girls have a birthmark on their ear. I noticed it when I helped hang all of these, but I never understood why. Interesting, isn't it?"

"Yes, it is." Carol said, as she looked closer. "I wonder why she added the birthmark to each one."

"I know why." Sarah replied with a smile. "She was painting my mother. She painted her as she grew up. All these paintings are dated November 3rd. That was my mother's birthday. My mother had a birthmark on her ear."

Chapter Twenty Three

.

They sat down to lunch in the huge dining room as Nancy brought Mr. Howard in to join them. He looked much better now that he had rested. She turned to leave the room, but he asked her to join them.

"Nancy has been like a member of our family." He explained to his guests as he turned to her and continued. "I want to tell the whole story, and I want her to hear it, too."

"Thank you, Mr. Howard." Nancy smiled and took a seat near him.

"I've made important decisions all my life, and I've never looked back or regretted any of them, except for one. And, that one was a big one. I never should have taken the baby from Samantha. I've known it for years, but I never would admit it, to myself, or anyone. At the time, I thought I had to do it. I thought I had no choice. But, I was wrong."

"I am an old man now, and I need to try to set things right." His food went untouched as he started to talk. "Sarah, I know without a doubt that you are my great-granddaughter, and I am very happy that you are here."

Sarah felt the corners of her eyes fill with tears as she watched this old man open up and swallow years of pride.

"Samantha was just seventeen when she became pregnant. I was furious and couldn't even think straight. Ellen, my dear wife, tried to talk to me about it, but I wouldn't listen. When I found out the father was the son of my competitor and enemy, I was even more determined to send the baby away. My pride got in the way, and I did a horrible thing. Now that I sit here and look at this beautiful young woman, I realize how much I lost by sending my only grandchild away. You see, Samantha was my only child and she never married

159

and she never had another child."

Benjamin Howard told the story of how he took Alexis to his attorney and instructed him to send the baby to a foster home using only her first name. He told how he sent Samantha and Virginia to Europe, hoping she would forget about the baby. He told about the crash of the stock market and how Sarah's other great-grandfather, John Thomas, and her grandfather, Alexander Thomas, had killed themselves just before Alexis was born.

As Sarah listened to this amazing story, it all fell into place. What she had learned in the past few days would take some time to absorb.

John, Carol, and Sarah shared their part of the story and told Benjamin and Nancy all they knew about Alexis and Harvey, the foster homes, her suicide and his tragic death. They all instinctively knew they should leave out any mention of child abuse. It served no purpose now. They told them how they had become Sarah's legal guardians and moved to Oregon.

As all the pieces fell into place, they grew more and more comfortable with one another, and by the end of the day, Benjamin Howard had a smile on his face and a twinkle in his eyes. Sarah had won his heart. This gruff old man had shown his softer side that Nancy had not seen since Samantha's death. Sarah was the best medicine available for this old man.

"Sarah, there are several boxes of my daughter's personal things that we kept in her apartment all these years. I just couldn't part with any of them and now I know why. They were meant for you. I want you to have her things. You are welcome to go through her rooms and take what you want."

"Thank you, Mr. Howard." Sarah smiled.

"And, by the way, Sarah, I think it's time you called me Grandpa."

Sarah was eager to spend time in that fascinating section of the mansion, but John and Carol insisted they should go back to their hotel and rest. It had been another very emotional day, and they were concerned, not only about Sarah, but about tiring Mr. Howard.

Nancy told them he had a stroke just after Samantha was killed, and his health had deteriorated since that time. They didn't want him to get overly tired, and besides, he needed time to absorb all of this. In one day he learned that his daughter had known the whereabouts of her baby, that his granddaughter had killed herself and that he had a great-granddaughter. It was a lot for an old man.

Sarah tossed and turned that night. The portrait of her grandmother stayed in her head and the memories of her pretty face at the funeral haunted her. What if she would have talked to Sarah and Harvey that day? How would that have changed their lives? What if Harvey hadn't gone to meet Jackson that night? Would he still be alive? If Samantha hadn't attended his funeral, she wouldn't have been traveling those treacherous roads in the winter, and she would still be alive.

What if she had talked to Sarah at Harvey's funeral? Maybe Sarah would have gone to live with her in Seattle. But if she had, she wouldn't have had those years with John and Carol. The "what ifs" rolled around and around in her head until she was exhausted, and she forced herself to stop thinking about them. She had to accept the chain of events that had brought her to this point in her life and make the best of it.

As sleep drifted toward Sarah, it occurred to her that she had been blessed. She had lost loved ones, but she had gained other loved ones, and now she had a great- grandfather. She was anxious to learn more about him and her grandmother, Samantha, and she would start learning in the morning. She fell into a deep sleep with a smile on her face.

She was the first one to wake the next morning and was completely showered and dressed by seven o'clock. She waited impatiently while John and Carol got ready for the day.

"Relax, Honey." John told her as he watched her fidget, "We can't very well show up at the Howard Mansion this time of day. We will take our own car this time, stop and have breakfast, and be there about ten o'clock."

"I'm just so anxious to get started. It is such a fascinating place, and I get to go through my grandmother's personal things. I can't wait!"

Nancy opened the massive door as they approached. Benjamin

Howard was waiting in the foyer, in his wheelchair, as they entered. He invited them to join him for some coffee in the garden, and though Sarah was anxious to get started with the project, she also wanted to get to know her great-grandfather, so she joined the others.

Benjamin was full of life and seemed years younger than he had the day before. He took control of the conversation immediately and told them stories of Samantha and his wife, Ellen. He was obviously very proud of them and asked Nancy to bring the family albums, so he could show them off to his guests.

Two hours went by, and they were still looking at old photo albums and listening Benjamin Howard's stories when Nancy interrupted them and told them lunch was being served. Sarah couldn't believe how the time had rushed by. She was fascinated by her great-grandfather's stories of Samantha and Ellen, but felt sad that she would never have the opportunity to meet them. After lunch was finished, Nancy told their guests that Mr. Howard needed to have some time for rest, and even though he claimed he was not tired, she wheeled him away to his room. When she returned, John and Carol told Nancy they thought it was best for them to leave, as they didn't want to wear out their welcome in the Howard Mansion. But, Nancy was adamant that they should stay in the Howard home.

"We have so many rooms that are just sitting empty. It is silly for you to pay for a hotel. Besides, Mr. Howard wants to see as much of Sarah as he can. This will be best for everyone."

John and Carol were hesitant, but Sarah was immediately convinced that Nancy was right.

"Oh please, let's stay here!" She said with enthusiasm. "It is so beautiful, and I would like to have some time to go through my grandmother's things."

"I suppose it will be alright, John." Carol looked to him for approval. "Sarah does need some more time here."

"Yes, please stay, Mr. Peterman. May I suggest you and Mrs. Peterman go check out of your hotel, and I will have your room ready for you when you return. In the meantime, Sarah can spend some time in Samantha's apartment."

"I suppose that makes sense, as long as you are sure it is not too much trouble, Nancy?" John questioned.

"It is no trouble at all, Mr. Peterman, and believe me, Mr. Howard will be thrilled to have a captive audience for his stories." Nancy smiled, and the three guests laughed, knowing it was hard to get away once he started his stories. But, each one secretly looked forward to hearing more from him.

John and Carol left for the hotel, and Sarah looked at Nancy with raised eyebrows, and a look that gave away her thoughts.

"Sarah, I already know what you are thinking. Come on. There is no reason to keep you waiting any longer. Let's go to Samantha's apartment."

Nancy unlocked the door and said, "Take all the time you want, Sarah. I'll be in my room if you need anything."

Sarah felt a sense of elation as she slowly entered the lovely and spacious apartment. She took a deep breath as she closed the door behind her and surveyed the dark room. The heavy draperies were tightly drawn so she immediately opened them to expose a panoramic view of the city and Puget Sound. The earlier visit to the apartment with Nancy, John, and Carol had not done the room justice. They had only looked at the paintings with the overhead light. Now, Sarah saw the full effect of the lovely apartment.

The room, now flooded in sunlight, was so obviously one that had belonged to a woman. It was tastefully decorated with a feminine touch. Sarah loved everything about it. She immediately felt at home and spent the first few minutes just walking around and touching the beautiful things.

The apartment consisted of a living room, bedroom, bathroom, den and tiny kitchen. The walls were painted in a lovely cream color that made the rooms feel bright and homey, with just the right touches of European accents. And, of course, the walls were covered with the paintings.

Sarah had to admit that even though the paintings were very good, they made her uncomfortable. She still felt uneasy about her mother, and somehow, Samantha had been able to capture the captivating blue eyes of Alexis, even though she had not seen her baby since birth. Sarah tried to avoid the pictures of the older Alexis. They stirred bad memories. She continued to touch things and get acquainted with the living room, looking in drawers and cabinets, for more than an hour before she realized she had not found the boxes of personal things her great-grandfather had mentioned.

She made her way into the bedroom and her eyes were drawn to a photograph of a young man, who looked to be in his early twenties, on the nightstand next to the canopy bed. She picked up the old framed picture and studied the handsome man. She thought there was a slight resemblance to Alexis, and after looking closely, she saw the familiar birthmark on his ear. This man was her grandfather. This was Alexander Thomas. This was the man who had killed himself, rather than face his financial problems.

She sat on the edge of the bed and held the picture. Her mother, her grandfather and her great-grandfather had all killed themselves. It seemed Sarah came from a long line of people who would rather die than deal with adversity. It made her mad! The more she thought about it, the madder she got. She was their descendant, but she wasn't like them. She refused to be like them! She had faced adversity and she had never thought of killing herself. What a cowardly thing to do!

She was still sitting on the bed, trying to understand what caused a person to make that horrible and final decision, when she heard a tap on the door.

"Hi, Honey." Carol peaked her head in the doorway of the bedroom. "I hope I'm not disturbing you, but we just got back from checking out of the hotel. I wanted to see how things are going."

"Okay." Sarah said. "Here, take a look at my grandfather." She handed the picture to Carol and continued. "I just can't understand why people commit suicide. My grandfather was young, with his whole life ahead of him, yet he killed himself. Wouldn't you think he would at least want to live for his baby? I mean, if his father was already dead, he could have married my grandmother and raised their baby together. I just don't understand."

"Sarah, I have never understood how a person could take their own life either, but we don't know the whole story. We can't possibly know all that went on in their minds, and we shouldn't judge them for what they did. We should feel compassion for them."

"It's pretty hard to feel compassion for my mother. All she ever did was hurt me. She was my mother, but she did nothing for me."

"I know it seems that way, Honey." Carol sat down on the bed next to her and put her arm around her. "But, your mother did do something for you. She brought you into this world and gave you the gift of life."

"Yeah, I know, but it makes me so angry that she left this legacy of suicide."

"I admit, that's not much of a legacy, but she did leave you something else, Sarah. Something that is very valuable."

"What's that?" Sarah asked with skepticism.

"The letters, Sarah. If she hadn't kept those letters, you would never have learned about your grandparents and your real father. And, you might still think Ben Jackson was responsible for Harvey's death. I would say those letters are a very big part of your legacy, and you should choose to focus on their value, and how they have impacted your life."

"You're right." Sarah said. "The letters have really changed my life, and I hadn't even realized how much until just now. Wow, I have a lot to be thankful for, don't I?"

"Yes, you do. Sarah, I want you to always remember, it is so easy to look for the negative side of any situation, but it is so much more productive to look for the positive side."

"You have always been so wise. I can't imagine my life without you and John. You have made me a better person, and I love you, very much."

"I love you, too, Sarah."

As they held each other and hugged tightly, it occurred to Sarah that she still hadn't found the boxes she had set out to find. She kept getting distracted. But, she was learning so much, and so many things were starting to make sense to her now. It had been an incredible few days.

Carol helped Sarah continue the search in the bedroom, and it didn't take long for them to find the boxes. The first box was filled with sketches of Paris and English landscapes, done by Samantha. Sarah was thrilled with her find, and even though she wanted to spend time looking at each sketch, she was anxious to see what else she could find so they continued to open the boxes of personal items.

They found stacks of letters from Ellen Howard to Samantha, and Sarah knew these letters would tell a story all by themselves. She couldn't wait to read them. The last box was very heavy, and Sarah squealed with delight as she opened it and removed the first of many leather-bound journals. Each journal had the name of Samantha Howard, with the year engraved in gold on the cover, and each page was filled with delicate handwriting.

"Oh my gosh!" Sarah cried. "These are my grandmother's journals. I can't believe she wrote in all of these." She pulled each journal out of the box and fanned through the pages.

Carol joined Sarah in removing the journals and stacking them on the bed. "There must be more than twenty journals here, Sarah. The earliest appears to be in 1929, and her mother, Ellen Howard, gave it to Samantha. Oh, listen to what was written on the inside cover."

My Darling Samantha,

Please remember we learn the most and become stronger because of the difficult times we face in our lives. You have suffered a great loss and my heart breaks because you are hurt. Try to put your thoughts into this journal and tell your story. Putting the words down on paper will help you heal. Time can heal all wounds, even the very deepest of wounds. I will always love you more than life, as I know you will always love Alexis.
Your Loving Mother
Ellen Howard
November 1929

"This was her first journal, and it looks like there is one for each year from then on."

Sarah was so touched that she felt the tears form in her eyes. "I'll be able to know my grandmother. I can read her thoughts as she wrote them down for all those years. What a wonderful gift!"

"It looks like you will finally have answers to all of your questions, Sarah. I'm sure these journals will tell a great story."

And, they did. Sarah learned the story of how her grandparents met and fell in love. She read about Samantha's baby being taken from her, and her years of endless search for her. The journals filled in the gaps for the years that her great-grandfather couldn't know about, like the years she spent in Europe, the friends she made, and the annual painting of her baby.

Sarah, John, and Carol spent three more days with Benjamin Howard and Nancy. They had been treated like royalty and made to feel that the Howard Mansion was their home, too. They promised to return for another visit as soon as they could find the time. In just a few short days, Sarah had grown very fond of her great-grandfather, and she promised him that she would visit often.

By the time Sarah finished reading the journals, she felt that she knew her grandmother, Samantha. She had grown to love her and respect her, and for the first time in her life, she felt a strong connection to her birth family. She finally understood how Alexis must have felt so alone and abandoned. If only she had known how much she had been loved, by Samantha. Her life could have been so different.

At eighteen years old, Sarah finally felt at peace with her mother. Now that she knew about Grandmother Samantha, Sarah realized she was very much like her, and she liked that. She was proud to be like Samantha Howard. Samantha Howard had forgiven her father for the terrible thing he had done. Sarah could finally forgive her mother.

One of the entries in the journal stood out to Sarah and she realized she had lived her life much like that of Grandmother Samantha. It read, "Never give up! You never know what tomorrow may bring".

Chapter Twenty Four

1976

Dr. Sarah Taylor settled into her first class seat on the United Airlines flight from Seattle to Boise. As the coach passengers boarded the plane and passed by, they couldn't help but notice the lovely lady with the captivating blue eyes. Everything about the woman said she was wealthy and polished, and the smile said she was a happy, friendly person.

As the flight took off, Sarah forced herself to relax and close her eyes. She would finally get to see the finished product and she was so excited, she could barely sit still. The flight would take an hour and one half, and the drive to the site would only be another couple of hours. She let her mind wander and reflect on the past eight years. My, how her life had changed. Again.

With the encouragement of John and Carol, Sarah had decided to study psychiatry, and now had her doctorate from the University of Oregon. She specialized in children's studies and now that her college years were behind her, she was finally able to concentrate on her long-term plan. She was on her way to Benton, Idaho.

Eight years of school seemed to drag on at the time, but now that she looked back, it hadn't been so bad. So much had happened.

She had spent many of her vacations and spring breaks visiting Grandpa Howard in Seattle and had grown to love him. He taught her so much about business and insisted she learn everything she could about the Howard Estate. He had died two years ago and Sarah was grateful she had those precious years with him. His will had bequeathed the entire Howard Estate to Sarah, with two exceptions.

He left instructions that his nurse, Nancy, be cared for the rest of her life and he also gave her enough money to buy a comfortable home in Seattle. And, a handsome sum was sent to Virginia Ellis Whittaker, in London, as a thank you for the years of service and friendship to his daughter, Samantha.

Sarah was overwhelmed with the amount of money that was left to her. She immediately asked John to take care of the finances. In addition, at the request of Sarah, John and Carol moved with her into the Howard Mansion in Seattle. Carol was busy redecorating and updating the huge home. John had retired from the bank so he could help Sarah with the Howard Estate. Sarah had decided to move into Samantha's old apartment.

She had big plans for the money she received, and with the help of John, a ten-year plan was already in place. She had more money than she could possibly use in her lifetime, and she intended to put it to good use.

The plane landed on time, and as Sarah walked off the plane, she was met by a young man, and escorted to the waiting car. She carried a fat briefcase and a purse, and he arranged to pick up the two suitcases that had been checked.

"I think you will be pleased with what you see, Dr. Taylor."

"I can't wait! It has been a long time coming."

"It sure has, but I'm sure you will see that it was worth the wait. Everything is first class and right on schedule. The grand opening is tomorrow at 1:00 P.M. and we already have a waiting list for the next one."

"That doesn't surprise me. I was hoping this project would be in great demand."

"Well, it sure it. And, I would like to tell you that I think you have done a great thing. You will make a difference in a lot of lives, you know."

"Thank you. That was always my plan."

They drove through the tiny town of Benton and headed toward the Snake River. The old familiar scent of the mint fields told Sarah they were close to their destination. They passed the Big Bend, and

Sarah took a deep breath. It was still hard to realize this was where her father had died. She turned her head to look down at the river until it was out of her sight. Looking forward, she knew she would soon be able to see what she had planned, worked and waited for, all these years.

And, then she saw it. The huge sign at the edge of the road read:

THE HOWARD HOME
"A Privately Funded Home For Children"

The car turned down the lane, now widened and paved with asphalt, and Sarah saw the finished product. Where once stood the old home place was now a new brick building, three stories high, over-looking the Snake River. The old barn and cellar had been removed and had been replaced with a lovely park full of playground equipment, benches, fountains, trees, flowers, and walkways. The entire twenty acres had been transformed into a beautiful, safe haven for children.

The facility would accommodate one hundred children, of all ages, and had private rooms for the thirty faculty members and caregivers. Sarah, and the Howard Estate, had spared no expense with the design and construction. The Howard Home was beautiful!

She stood at the entrance of the building and smiled as she realized her dream had come true. The children would arrive tomorrow and she would be there to greet them.

This was just one of many homes that would be constructed to provide homes for unwanted and unloved children. This had been her plan for the twenty acres since she learned it belonged to her. Her Grandfather Howard's estate had made it all possible and she knew he would be proud.

Tomorrow would be a special day. John and Carol would be with her for the grand opening. Ben Jackson, who was now the mayor of Benton, would help Sarah cut the ribbon. Nancy, who had taken on the role of an aunt to Sarah, had promised to attend. And, Sarah had sent an invitation to Virginia and Henry Whittaker in England. They had responded immediately. They would love to meet the granddaughter of their old friend, Samantha, and would be at the grand opening before continuing on to Seattle for a visit to Virginia's family.

Taking a deep breath, Sarah opened the door and walked into the foyer. A huge portrait of an eight-year-old Sarah Taylor hung on the wall. The long blonde hair had ribbons to match her dress and the artist had captured the intensity of those huge, blue eyes. A bronze plaque, just below the painting, was engraved with the following words:

My home is your home
May you always feel welcome
May you always feel loved

Sarah Taylor